Immortal Wars

Rita Sanborn

For my children, I would start a riot for you.

The Fire

People referred to that night in 2038 as the Night of the Fire, or simply the Fire. Ruth Anderson Guzman heard the phrase, the Fire, whispered with awe or contempt towards her, until he, her captor, would silence the room with his withering stare or just with his mere presence. His anger erupted at the mention of the Fire, threatening those nearest but especially menacing Ruth. In the early years, Ruth suffered greatly from his outbursts, punishing her repeatedly for that night, that fire.

Both of them, Ruth and her captor, were there that night when the fire occurred. Ruth dreamt almost nightly of that day; the events looped over and over in her brain. She was helpless to stop the dreams, just as she was helpless to stop the events of that night.

The irony was that the fire did much to wreak havoc to LIFETECH and destroy Ruth's life, but it only damaged a portion of the building as the fire damage was isolated to the interior of the second floor. Ruth did not see the start of the fire or the aftermath. She recalled, though, vividly the moments of that day leading up to the fire.

Early that evening, Ruth and Marco took Molly over to Michael's home after a full day of work at LIFETECH. It was a forty-minute ride on the public transit to Michael's home. Six-year-old Molly shook with excitement as she rode transit; this was a rare occasion for Molly, especially in the evening so close to her bedtime. Usually, Ruth avoided to take Molly on public transit due to fear. The news reported daily of muggings and assaults. Marco tried to explain that the reports were exaggerated to drum up fear, that thousands of people rode public transit with no issue every day. Ruth was not convinced and she planned to avoid public transit as much as she could.

That day, though, Ruth recalled vividly the enormous smile on Molly's face, how Molly bounced up and down, moving to Ruth's and then Marco's lap. Ruth hung on to the memory of Molly's soft small body and the sensation of wrapping her own arms around the small child. At Michael's small house, Ruth barely had a chance to kiss Molly goodbye. Molly ran off to find her cousin, so excited to have an impromptu sleepover.

Hours later, Ruth and Marco snuck into LIFETECH, specifically the server rooms on the second floor. Ruth's role was to get them — Marco and three others — into LIFETECH and the server rooms. It seemed to go smoothly. They entered the building after eleven pm as planned, bypassing the security guards. Ruth and Marco had spent months of studying the guard rotation to prepare for this night. Ruth and Marco were tasked with server room two. Ruth was almost giddy with the adventure, sneaking past the front security, using the stolen access cards. Up to this moment, she felt nausea with fear but they made it past the guards now.

Marco and Ruth entered the server room. As the door closed, Marco turned to her and kissed her passionately.

"We do this for Molly, eh?" Marco whispered fiercely.

They went to work. Marco took the USB stick from his pocket and attached it to the main frame. This would upload the virus the resistance created. The others were in server room one, with the same task. Ruth kept watch near the door, keeping it open a crack so she could peer into the hallway. She waited as Marco attached the hard drive to the server's main frame. The upload started, 5%, 12%. Time seemed to have slowed down and the tension was building. All they had to do was to ensure the upload was complete and then they could leave. Ruth was not even sure what the virus would do. Stop LIFETECH; this was the goal that Marco and his group risked their lives to achieve. Ruth realized, after a lifetime of living within the rules, of playing it safe, she was risking it all tonight. She hoped it was worth it.

78% uploaded. They heard a ruckus in the hall. Is it from the other server room? Hurry up, Ruth willed the hard drive. She could barely look at Marcus; it was too much for her, too dangerous. Her heart was pounding in her chest; she felt lightheaded. A wave of nausea returned, stronger now, as she closed the door and prayed that they would remain undiscovered.

"Stop! Lay down!" Two armed security guards broke through the door.

"Get down! Get down!"

Marco grabbed at one of the guards. Their two bodies collided with the electronic equipment, processors, and servers. Ruth heard the two grunting. Ruth was screaming now. She heard gunshots; the sound magnified in the small space of the room. Marco collapsed. The guards moved in on his prone body, kicking and stomping.

"Marco! Stop it! Stop it!" Ruth screamed, and a guard moved towards her, swinging a baton. The first hit was across her jaw. Then the blows hit her all over, up and down her body. She could not defend herself or help Marco. She dropped into a fetal position against the wall, seeing Marco on the ground beside her, crumbled and still. Blood was everywhere. She tried to reach out to him. A faceless guard stomped on her shoulder and arm over and over. He kicked her repeatedly, making contact with her back and hips. The pain was intense, shooting throughout.

That man, the face of LIFETECH, hovered above them, pale and alien.

"Marco. Marco." Ruth whimpered and then everything went black.

Ruth woke to find her broken body dropped into a chair. She was now in an office, one she did not recognize. The guards tied Ruth to the chair so that her body did not slide off. Pain throughout her body was so encompassing that she has no control. She could not move.

"Give me names of who else was involved." The man, her future captor, kicked her broken leg, and she screamed.

"Talk, you bitch."

"Talk." He screamed, and she felt his hot breath on her face. He slapped her hard across her temple over and over. Everything grew black again, and he faded from her sight.

When Ruth woke again, the fire was in full swing. From the back office, where she was held, she saw nothing except black smoke wafting in from under the chair. Fire alarms wailed in the hallway. The room filled with the smoke and she gagged and sputtered. Security guards grabbed her, rough, and dragged her out of LIFETECH. She saw her body, limp. Her leg and arm bent unnaturally beneath her.

"Where is Marco?" she moaned. A coughing fit hit her and when it subsided, she asked again. No one answered. No one looked at her. She was dragged outside the building and shoved in a van. She thought it was a van. Ruth's ears were now ringing with the sounds of several emergency vehicles — the fire and police. Voices were shouting. Red and blue lights reflected on the walls in the van, swirling with the siren wails.

"Marco." Ruth croaked his name, but no one was there to hear her. She felt the vehicle lurch forward. If she wasn't in so much pain, Ruth would have felt fear, more fear than she had ever experienced before that night.

The image of Marco collapsed on the server room floor seared in her mind. Now her imagination added hot, angry flames devouring Marco.

Chapter 1

Ruth found herself, like thousands of other days before, nested in a sea of white bedding, pillows crumpled beneath her, as the wave of artificial white light seeped in the room and the sound of birdsong grew from a whisper to a conversation. She reluctantly woke, unwilling leaving the haven of her unconscious world of sleep with its ghosts of dreams and long — ago past images fading. Her arm and shoulder ached from the weight of her sleeping body. Ruth favoured her left side even after all this time that had passed since her injuries had healed. It was on the left side where she sustained a broken femur, pelvis, and collarbone. Her mind was still foggy, not recalling where she was or who she was. It was a blissful moment that happened each day. Rising from the forgetfulness of the unconscious, alive and mostly awake but not fully remembering or aware. Then the bliss quickly dissipates when her consciousness crosses an invisible line and she recalled clearly where she was -- and who she was. This moment often happened at the end of the programed morning alarm, which began playing bird songs as it gradually increased the artificial light, designed to simulate daybreak until the light was at full brightness.

Like thousands of other mornings, Ruth reluctantly rose out of bed. She long established a habit of sleeping in the nude after decades of fussing with the constraints of nightclothes. The waist band that left a red mark; the fabric aggravated her restless legs. Modesty was long abandoned — in her bedroom, at least. She was certain, for the most part, that he had tired of monitoring her by now.

Ruth walked across the large room, devoid of colour except for the drawings and art supplies she kept on the dresser. She stood in front of the large window and pressed the control for the window shade so she could scan the open grounds below and the sky above. The rooms — a bedroom, bathroom, and small sitting room — assigned to her as her living quarters were up on the third floor.

First, she surveyed the sky, a blue cloudless sky with a small burning disc of pale yellow. Crows and magpies swooped in flocks from right to left. Their cries were angry — far from the songlike chirping of her morning program. Below was a large lawn of bright green, almost fraudulent in appearance, lined by uniformed trees in the distance. A small rumble reached her window as she spotted the gardener riding the lawnmower, creating a precise criss-cross pattern. They wore a large-brimmed hat and the grey overalls worn by the labourers on the compound. The trees in the distance hid the iron gate and the security patrols. Their uniforms were utilitarian black with a small shoulder patch of white, SECURITY printed in bold black letters.

Ruth headed to the private bathroom to the left of the bed, near the bedroom door, and began her ablutions. With mechanical habit, she brushed her teeth, not looking in the giant crystal-clear mirror hanging in front. The mirror glowed with a soft artificial light from within, magnifying every detail of her face, and she had to make a considerable effort to avoid meeting her own solemn grey eyes. The effect was having a silent intruder in the bathroom, intent on avoiding her as she avoided them.

Ruth moved into the shower and stood there for several moments, head hung low, letting the sonic pressure beat on her neck, shoulders, and back. She had the temperature up as high as she could physically stand it. As the painful heat pricked her, the plexiglass of the shower cubicle fogged opaque, the air thick and moist. She watched her skin on her belly and legs redden. Beads of water appeared out of the air, then slid down with gravity. Eventually, she mustered the energy to wash and rinse her hair and scrub her body clean. She stepped out, her body quickly drying as the water evaporated. She wrapped a towel around her head and performed the daily moistening ritual: shins first, up the thighs, hips and back, finishing with each arm. There was no rush, no place to run to. Time did not matter.

Ruth now found herself in front of the full-length mirror in the bedroom. She could not ignore the woman before her. The mirror glowed softly, but the image before her was stern and disapproving. She combed her damp hair straight back. Her face, reflected in the mirror, was devoid of expression, almost inhuman. She worked for a long time to perfect that emotionless expression, one that would help hide her thoughts from him and the others. It was the key to survival in this house, in this world.

Ruth was of average height for a female and average weight; her long habit of exercise, though, had strengthened her body as her muscles were hard and sinewy like granite. Her skin was pale and smooth, as she, like most, avoided the harsh, damaging sun. Ruth rarely went outside nowadays except for her daily two-hour run, and she ensured she was completely covered up. As she stared at this pale woman with dark eyes and hair — a revenant, a ghoul, a faded spirit — she felt detached, numb. This body was a stranger to her, though she knew every mark and scar on it. Ruth stared at this stranger, wondering who will blink first. The dark eyes stared back, not revealing anything. Then she dressed in a grey long-sleeved top and running pants, designed for UV protection. She took several deep breaths and centred herself with a couple of old yoga poses she learnt a lifetime ago.

Next step was the digi-medic, the digital medical analyzer. She had to stand in front of the scanner, beside the bedroom door, while it scanned her body from head to toe. Then she offered her hand reluctantly to the machine, and it pricked her finger. Based on its analysis of a drop of her ruby red blood, the digi-medic would dispense daily supplements and medication as required. The digi-medic then tailored the meals of the day based on its findings. Often, she was presented with iron rich meals, much more food that she would want to eat, but she knew the outcome if she tried to avoid the supplements and the food. The trickier part was to avoid the medications the digi-medic determined she needed through the scans and the monthly psychological examinations by the in-house physicians. She had to remain calm, control her heartbeat, and then force a smile on to her face and in the tone of her voice. Think happy thoughts, she repeated to herself as a mantra. But happy thoughts were difficult. She often thought of the laughter of children, sounds of the playground. Sensations such as the feel of a small hand in hers or the sugary powdery smell of a child's hair. The thoughts had to be vague and generalized. *Do not open doors you cannot handle, Ruth*, she warned herself. Happy thoughts could be dangerous.

It took decades to master the digi-medic. Before this, the digi-medic and the medical staff determined Ruth was at risk to herself and the medical staff heavily sedated her. Ruth lost herself to the drug induced fog. This was during the first years, after she emerged from a medically induced a coma and was still recovering from that injury. Then, many years passed and she spent them in that thick heavy fog, barely able to get out of bed because of the drug induced stupor.

Ruth drifted through the heavy fog for a long time until the digi-medic diagnosed the level of sedation, with the accompanying risks to her cardiovascular system and the significant decrease in muscle strength, as harmful. The dosage was reduced. Slowly she woke from the numbing stupor and realized she, beyond reason, still had a will to survive and a desire to fight back.

A knock at the door startled Ruth from her stand off with the digi-medic. She moved to open the door to her suite. It was a servant with the digi-medic determined breakfast meal, based on yesterday's results. The older woman — grey hair streaking her head and wrinkles straining around her eyes — rolled in the cart with the meal tray with a carafe of hot sweet tea and a pitcher of water. She spoke no words to Ruth but took a moment to stare defiantly into Ruth's face. Both women were a similar height, with dark hair and eyes. Ruth, though, stood straight with an athletic build in her pristine monotone outfit, her pale face glowing with health. The older woman stood stooped at the shoulders, her uniform washed out to a faded blue with ancient stains. Her face bore the marks of sun damage and worry lines.

Ruth gave up attempts at polite interactions long ago in this household, except for a quiet 'thank you' or a 'please'. Without a spoken word about her within earshot, they all appeared to label her as traitor, as an other. All of them — the labourers, the servants, the morts — seemed to despise her. Throughout the years, the decades, she saw the anger and disgust in their eyes. Ruth was enslaved to his whims, controlled and caged, but they only saw her pristine clothes, the abundance of food, and the luxury of her living space.

"Thank you." Ruth said in a soft, even tone, avoiding the older woman's angry face. The morts seemed to display their anger only openly to Ruth. If they dared to display their anger and resentment to the others — well, there were real consequences for them if they just irritated the others or proved to be an inconvenience.

Ruth had long established a routine to combat the tedium of time: the ritual of rising and showering, the digi-medic, reading as she ate breakfast in her sitting room, and stretches and core activities to help loosen her muscles and relieve the phantom pain from that injury long ago. Daily, Ruth completed sets of push-ups and planks to build strength and meditation to keep her emotions at bay. Then she settled in several hours of copying or scribing — a funny ancient term. At lunch time, another cart was wheeled in and the old cart wheeled out. Ruth reluctantly paused in her scribing. She was subjected to more hostile stares from the older woman. The mort woman would look with disgust at the stacks of paper and the orderly lines of blue pens. Blue ink was Ruth's preference.

Near mid afternoon, Ruth would finish her work, tidying up the supplies and place her transcriptions, a slim stack of paper in the ancient 8 x 10 letter size, into the desk by the great window in her sitting room. She drank a glass of water and donned her running shoes and sun hat. Then she headed out for her daily run.

For the most part, they allow her a fair amount of freedom to move about. A driver and vehicle could be requested only during the long periods when he was off the compound and if Melissa Hammel or the other assistants were in a benign mood. He often took trips that lasted weeks or months. He never told her any details -- no one did -- but Melissa Hammel, his senior personnel assistant, would let slip some information when addressing security or housekeeping. Ruth had to ensure she took most of her supper meals down in the great hall so she could gather some information, preferably when Alan Blackmore was away, like this week. When he was away, the atmosphere was less oppressive and everyone, herself included, would breathe with more ease.

To head out for a run, Ruth would report to security by the great door, the main entrance. She indicated where she planned to run and when she would return. In the past, Ruth had an escorted each time she left the compound — an imposing figure in black, running behind her in order to report her every action to him — but the mort security did not have the luxury of time like her to develop their fitness. Ruth ran so much and for long periods of time, and as such, she became a strong and swift runner. She wore out more of the security staff who trailed behind her than she could count. The digi-medic ensured she had the optimal nutrition. These two factors, practice and nutrition, made Ruth too fast for the mort security to keep up with. She did not know any of the others that ran like she did, though there must be some others out there in other compounds. The others here relied on the fitness centre and its army of electronic circuits and concoctions of performance drugs to keep themselves fit with minimal effort or will power. The others did, though, display many compulsive obsessive tendencies, and some of them manifest those in obsessions through extreme sports or physical challenges. He, Alan Blackmore, was not obsessed with fitness. He manifested his obsessive traits in his fascination with Ruth, his empire, LIFETECH, and controlling those around him.

Chapter 2

Ruth ran out the gate. The gardener she observed earlier on the riding lawnmower was now trimming the grass at the base of the fence line. They were currently near the gatehouse. The grass trimmer noisily crashed against metal and stone. She noticed the gardener was a mort man with dark hair and a stocky build. He looked directly at her for a long moment. Unless Ruth was mistaken, his eyes were more curious than hostile. This idea slowed her pace, and she unconsciously formed a tight smile towards him. The guard, another mort male with a clearly irritated expression that peered over the rims of dark sunglasses, motioned for Ruth to exit the gate so he could resume his post. She passed through the gate, not daring to look back.

Ruth picked up the pace and ran towards a dirt trail in the woods. It was a hot, stifling day under the cloudless sky with no breeze, but her outfit was designed to keep her body cool and comfortable. Her sun hat kept the fierce sunlight off her face and neck. She still felt perspiration quickly form on her back and chest and under her arms and knees and her pale skin redden with the physical exertion. She was free, though. Running set her free. She could shake the cautious restraint she held in the compound where hidden surveillance cameras watched her throughout. She knew satellites and drones overhead sometimes tracked her movements, but she could escape its observation while she ran through the woods.

Suddenly, a large buzzing sound startled her. A drone was flying behind her. She laughed and continued. The woods were too thick for it to follow her.

I thought he was on his yearly trip to inspect the Antarctic super server. He should not be back until next week. The others have shown no interest in me in decades, so what is this? She wondered if things were shifting back to her.

Throughout the years, the others' interest in her waxed and waned, mostly waning now. She was not that interesting to them, and she strongly encouraged that point of view with her highly regimented routine and her lack of engagement in the last century. He, Alan Blackmore, however, still focused his attention on her, treating her like a caged pet mouse. He, however, did not maintain his focus consistently. His other obsessions beckoned to him such as his need to travel the globe to ensure his seat of power among the other corporations.

She could no longer hear the drone. It was just her in the woods now. She saw flickers of movement as insects flew in the shafts of light. Birds were singing up in the trees and squirrels or chipmunks chattered in the shadows, warning others of her presence. The others did not enjoy the high heat of the day and the morts were labouring or in their settlements away from the compound and the other compounds owned by the others. The heat and the patrol vehicles on the roads surrounding the woods and the compounds kept the morts away.

Ruth figured the nearest settlement was less than five kilometres away. It was the former suburb of Richmond, and she was heading to its outskirt. The old city of Vancouver was further north. It was like most North American cities which were abandoned by the halted centuries ago and now inhabited by the extremely poor, all morts. Morts tried to settle in the suburbs or mort communities to avoid the lawlessness and the lack of employment the cities offered. Europe still maintained cities, as Ruth remembered from decades ago. The others there pushed out the morts with high rental rates and closing public transportation. The overall effect was similar — the separation of other from mort.

Four kilometres into her run and the woods thinned out; the ground dipped into a small gully with a creek running through it. It once was a large river, but like most of the bodies of water in the area, it was slowly drying up. It would have completely disappeared, but some of the halted turned their attention from their constant obsession with youth and vanity to the global warming crisis about two hundred years ago and created an environmental global net that helped slow down carbon build up and controlled precipitation, stalling the desertification of vast areas. Without this global net, this complete area would be inhospitable — a wasteland like the southern states.

The other side of the gully continued to thin out. Her cover was fading, so she guarded her actions again. It was unlikely that they could observe her, but not impossible. Her reprieve could end any moment now and she had a long-term plan she was not ready to abandon. Before the woods completely ended at an intersection near the mort settlement of Richmond, she lingered under the trees and grabbed the package of paper she had hidden in the sleeve of her shirt, wrapped in plastic. The plastic was wet and sticky from her sweat. Inside were twenty-five pages of carefully copied text. Today's text was copied from an old high school science textbook she found in the data library. It was a mix of rudimentary mechanical and engineering concepts written in her carefully crafted cursive. She took the paper out of the plastic and hid it in a fallen tree trunk she had seen the mort children playing by. The tree trunk served as home base to a wide game the children played, similar to kick the can.

The time was ten minutes to four o'clock and the local mort school bell would ring soon. Groups of the mort children would walk kilometres to their homes — usually small duplex houses and old brick apartments — the older children holding the hands of the younger ones. The young children, who did not need hands held, would skip and jump, and run circles around the older ones, who kept a wary eye out for the group. Barely teenagers, those older children lost the innocence of youth, knowing too well the dangers of the whims of the others. The others commissioned the schools and allowed mort children some basic education, but the others could easily close the school and the settlement housing to make room for another compound or resort. The older children likely now understood that they were vulnerable to being snatched up and forced to work in either of those. Ruth also heard rumours of others who targeted children to abduct for reasons Ruth did not want to think about. However, the other community had some limits, and they dispatched the ones who were truly heinous. These predators were never heard from again.

Ruth did not wait today for the school bell. She headed to the ocean another kilometre away to run along the hard packed sand. Seagulls flew all around her, screeching into the ocean winds. The ocean was calm today. Its pale blue nearly matched the sky above. A few boats dotted the horizon. She circled back and ran the six kilometres back to the Blackmore compound. She saw the children walking back to their housing; one or both of their parents were likely still labouring at the compounds or pulling shifts at the resorts or spas or even at the regional utilities. There were also a few factories in this area that the morts worked at. Some morts worked at the corporations such as LIFETECH. The corporations often providing better salaries and some benefits like access to doctors and dentists.

Snippets of youthful voices hung in the air: a laugh, a protest, an older child soothing hurt feelings — beautiful like the birdsongs that woke her each morning. Ruth wanted to linger, but she had to press on. She wiped the sweat away from her forehead. It stung her eyes as it mixed with the salty ocean mist. Ruth picked up her pace. She wanted to ensure she made the supper hour at the compound. She knew she needed to keep on top of the activities there and his plans. Alan Blackmore had been quiet for a while now, but Ruth knew it was too good to last.

At the compound, she quickly showered again and changed. She combed her hair into a ponytail and dressed in an unremarkable pair of pants and a white top. In the great hall, Alan Blackmore's household of servants and assistants gathered to eat the evening meal. It was a skeleton crew of twelve this evening. The rest were with Alan Blackmore in the Antarctic, the last stop on his voyage. Other workers were on the job — cooking in the kitchens, making the security rounds and countless other tasks the others paid little attention to. Melissa was there, though, dressed in a red dress and impractical high-heeled boots. Melissa wanted to stand out. She was the boss in his absence, and she wanted to ensure everyone knew. There were only a few others in the room that were not morts. Technically they were, like Ruth, immortals or halted. Their aging processes halted decades or centuries ago by LIFETECH technology, the coveted process that kept LIFETECH on top in the global consortium of tech corporations that dominated the globe politically and economically.

Rob McDonald and Maury Poirrier were halted close to the time Ruth was. At that time, the two men were minor players in Alan Blackmore's company, but both proved to be useful to him. Both had excellent coding skills. Rob McDonald had a phenomenal understanding of genetics and the markers for aging. Maury Poirrier was ruthless in the laboratory and did whatever was asked, including conducting thousands of unethical experiments on animals and the homeless. Without these two, Alan could not have realized his dream of immortality.

Melissa was a recent addition about fifty years ago. Alan plucked her from the staff at one of his resort properties in the interior, attracted to her large blue eyes, auburn ringlets, and her smooth youthful face. Reaching barely five feet in height, Melissa appeared years younger than the age of twenty-one when she was halted. She was a very healthy specimen for a former mort.

Ruth avoided Rob and Maury with all her effort. She would have to be desperate for information if it forced her to interact with them. She had several interactions with those two in the past, and it did not go well for her. Rob and Maury were cruel and calculating, like Alan. Melissa though, Ruth could manage her. She was easily influenced and, though she hated to admit to anyone or to herself, Melissa saw Ruth first as a potential ally in the compound and second as a mother figure. Morts often had limited interaction with their parents, as their parents had to work long hours in order to provide for their children. Melissa was particularly needy for parental figures. It was apparent how she often looked at Alan, eager to please.

Ruth slid behind Melissa in line for the evening buffet. When Alan was away, the offerings were not as extravagant, but the food was plentiful and fresh. Melissa did not notice Ruth as she was busy giving instructions to her mort assistant, a slight man about thirty.

"Be sure to prepare Mr. Blackmore's quarters by Thursday. I don't expect him to arrive until Saturday, but I don't want to be caught unprepared in case he returns a day early." Melissa spoke to the slight man, her back towards Ruth.

Her assistant nodded; his posture slouched towards her in deference, and he frowned in concentration as he took notes. He looked like a pale shadow of a human compared to Melissa's garish bright colours: red dress, pink skin, and painted face with lots of gold eyeshadow highlighting her bright blue eyes.

"Remind me tomorrow about the party. He wants to host his annual party in the next ten or days. Usual crew. We will need to start contacting their staff. Last minute, I know, but it's got to be done. Anyways, leave me now. I need to talk to the others. Be in my office first thing tomorrow." Melissa waved the mort assistant away, and he quickly departed before she could task him further.

Ruth had tried to make contact with this mort in the past. She tried to befriend him, or at least establish some kind of communication. She needed the avenues to keep informed. Someone must have warned this assistant about getting too close to her, as he would not acknowledge her or respond to any of her questions. Ruth could not push too hard, so she had to stop trying to engage him in conversation early on when he refused to speak to her. She had gotten the last one, Trevor Fisher, in trouble. He disappeared ten years ago when Alan Blackmore spotted them talking in a hall. Ruth did not want to think what happened to that mort; mort lives were disposable to the others.

"Ah Ruth, I would ask you how your day was, but I expect nothing new has occurred. Still only leaving your rooms to run." Melissa had turned around and finally noticed her, her tone arrogant. This was mostly for show for the morts and others in the great hall. Ruth doubted Melissa was aware that her tone and mannerisms were an imitation of Alan Blackmore, their great lord of the manor.

Melissa scanned Ruth, searching for any change, any clue. She knew Ruth was not like the others. Ruth was not a mort; rather, she was halted like the others, but she was here not by choice and she, although not outright imprisoned, was not free to leave. Ruth assumed Melissa must know some stories that lead up to her captivity at the Blackmore compound. It was unlikely that Melissa fully understood or appreciated the impact of what Ruth did to end up in this gilded cage, how Alan Blackmore would never forget. Alan would never give up his obsession with his pet mouse, as he called Ruth. No one spoke openly about Ruth or the night of the fire.

"Hello Melissa, I hope you are well." Ruth replied in a quiet, neutral voice, disregarding the smirk. Ruth needed to keep in Melissa's good books and not draw any close suspicion. She knew Melissa was drawn to her and wanted to hear about the long history from Ruth's own words. She needed an ally, too. Ruth also suspected Melissa was lonely, too. Again, in Melissa's presence, Ruth sensed

Melissa was drawn to her as an older mother like figure. Melissa was an other and always arrogant — sometimes cruel — but Melissa also had a vulnerability that revealed itself through the cracks of her carefully and liberally applied makeup. The only thing holding back Melissa from fully approaching Ruth was the acute awareness that those who appeared to collaborate with Ruth were ruthlessly punished or they disappeared like Trevor Fisher.

"So kind of you to inquire, Ruth. I want to warn you Alan is hosting a party in the next couple of days, and you will be expected to attend and be on time. Do not let your activities get in the way."

Against her inclinations to avoid Melissa and the others completely, Ruth took her plate of food and sat at the round table in the semiprivate dining area reserved for the others. The morts had a larger area, cafeteria style, similar to the one Ruth went to a lifetime ago when she attended university. Ruth usually sat by herself near the exit of the cafeteria, essentially in neither group. She tried to sit with the others a couple of times a week to gather what news she could. Even sitting near the morts proved to supply important news about what was going on outside the compound. Over the decades, she would hear rumblings of rebellions and insurgents. Last month she heard the morts talk about rising violence in the old city. The Council deployed their militia to suppress the morts.

Ruth made mental notes of the rising fractions: the mort rebellions, an other corporation trying to vie against Alan Blackmore's empire, prominent members in the Council. She tried to track all the relationships, such as who hated who or who was in bed with whom. Over the decades, the networks of human relations shifted, and Alan Blackmore and LIFETECH managed to remain at the top. At night, Ruth would jot cryptic notes in a hidden notebook to help her make sense of the world. She was looking for allies and vulnerabilities within the halted communities. So far, she had no luck, and she was too cautious to reach out beyond the pleasantries with Melissa.

When Ruth finally vacated the mental fog over two centuries ago and decided she wanted to survive, she also felt something else return — her need to resist. She needed to resist Alan Blackmore and the others and break free from here. Somehow, she wanted to help the mort children — those children who warily walked to and from the school every day, dreading when they too joined their parents as labourers for the others.

Tonight, the others were quiet, giving the impression of an amicable companionship — if Ruth had not known better. If given a decent chance, any of them would quickly betray the others to gain favour with Alan Blackmore. All three – Rob MacDonald, Maury Poirrier and Melissa Hammel --

sat, absorbed in the musings in their own heads. They had spent so much time together; no words were needed. The atmosphere in the Great Hall was different when Alan was there. They all then tripped over themselves, making small talk and trying to amuse Alan. Melissa, as the newest member of the halted, especially had the role of the jester or house fool. Tonight, several minutes passed in silence as the group had mostly eaten their meal. All three paused simultaneously to finish their assorted beverages. Again, digi-medic chose the appropriate supplements in the beverages.

"Mel, he's back on Saturday? Does he want to meet with Maury and me? I am still working out the coding for the next server upgrade. I told him it was not ready yet," Rob spoke, breaking the silence. He still maintained the Chief of Operations position in the company. He had fewer engineers under him and the morts lacked the skill set, purposely so. As such, he was the busiest of Alan Blackmore's staff.

Rob McDonald was a tall, slim man with unremarkable features. He rarely engaged with people other than Alan Blackmore and Maury Poirrier. Rob was quiet and reserved, preferring to fade into the background.

"Relax Rob. He has not asked about the upgrade yet. I think he is bored with travelling and the yacht."

"And of his paramour. What is her name?" Maury interrupted, "It's been a couple of years by now. He must be very bored with her."

Melissa flinched for a nanosecond; she once was his paramour. That relationship ended soon after Alan halted her. He then spent a year touring remote places by sea — South Asia, New Zealand, and Australia — leaving Melissa to stew in the compound. Melissa, essentially, was a survivor and knew she could not leave the gravy train that was Alan Blackmore. Melissa could not return to her mort community as a halted, so she took up the role as Alan's personal assistant with great enthusiasm. She did not look back. By now there was no mention about her time as Alan's paramour except in biting, cruel remarks by Rob and Maury. Rob and Maury did not press too hard with their remarks, they knew they should not throw rocks in glass houses. All of them were in the biggest glass house here at the Blackmore compound.

Maury Poirrier was an average built male appearing to be mid thirties. He had skinny arms with a middle age paunch. He vainly styled his massive head of hair in a duck's bill. It took several decades to fix his male pattern baldness after he was halted, and it never seemed to look quite right. It sat on his head like an ill-fitting wig. As cartoonish as he appeared, he was not a person to disregard or underestimate. Maury had a cruel streak before he was halted, and Ruth saw regularly he had no empathy or compassion. People were barely real to him, especially the morts. He shared this characteristic with Alan Blackmore. Unlike Alan, Maury was inherently lazy. Hence, he was more than comfortable to let Alan run the show.

Maury was the head of research and development. He led the scientists in their projects; projects that aimed to make the halted better, younger, and live forever. He conveyed Alan's wishes to the team, sometimes adding a few side projects of his own, and let the team get to work.

"Alan did mention that he expects you two to be at the party. The date will be confirmed when he returns. So don't make any other plans." Melissa added.

"Ah yes. What month is it? We are coming up on the anniversary of Alan's halt, right?" Maury replied. During the summer months, the party circuit started up. The halted community travelled between each other's estates and compounds and hosted lavish parties and events. Alan Blackmore often hosted a party in July to acknowledge the anniversary of his own halting.

"Yes, yes Mel. We know what is expected of us." Rob added.

Ruth noted it was ten days away from July 19th. Alan Blackmore did not note the anniversary every year, but this year marked a significant milestone, two hundred and fifty years since Alan and his crew were halted. LIFETECH was the winner in the immortality race, beating out several other corporations vying for immortality. The historic moment of LIFETECH defeating aging was the famous news conference on the 19th of July, 2038. The board and key members of LIFETECH underwent to the halting within that week.

Ruth was halted a month earlier than Blackmore and his staff when her body was trapped in a coma that was medically induced after her extensive injuries. She was the final test subject for the procedure that altered a human's DNA to stop the aging process. The procedure took less than a day to install the genetic recoding and then weeks later Ruth's DNA — Ruth was the earliest human subject — was successfully altered to halt aging. The digi-medics which monitored the health of the halted were designed in tandem to optimize the health of the halted. Two hundred and fifty years later, Ruth was biologically halted at the age of thirty years old.

After supper, Ruth ended the day back in her room, like she did most days. She scanned the internet for news, after an hour of laps in the compound swimming pool and yet another shower. Alan's company or the conglomeration of tech companies that governed the Americas and Europe, known as the Council, would heavily censor any news. As such, Ruth had to read between the lines. She looked for what was missing or the news she had to gather between the lines. After deciphering the probable reality from what was presented, Ruth updated her notebook. Sometimes she read an old novel. The trash that was written nowadays lacked any substance. Artificial Intelligence could turn out a better piece of art or literature from what most halted produced, but it still lacked a certain something. Ruth found AI literature unreadable, too.

The halted denied the morts freedom of artistic expression, except the occasional talented artist that was noticed and employed by the halted to decorate their homes and offices and to entertain them. Schools taught morts the basics so that they would be useful to the halted, but that was it. So, Ruth revisited the novels she read in her past life and then expanding into English literature or works translated into literature that she heard of when she was in university. She read all the works of several major writers such as Dickens, Atwood, Austen, the Brontes. She even tried to read Shakespeare, starting with the plays she studied in school. The evenings were long, and she needed to escape, if only in her mind.

After a few more stretches and mediation, Ruth crawled into bed. She tried to resist sleeping pills. No matter what the chemical composition was, they were habit forming and worsened her ability to fall asleep on her own. They also dulled her mind and reflexes, leaving her vulnerable at night. Since she started her physical regime of exercise, Alan Blackmore and the others left her alone mostly, but the whim might return and one of them might try to toy with her again. She had to wake swiftly to protect herself if one of them entered her room.

Mommy, Mommy, can I sleep with you and Daddy? The words of a long ago familiar voice entered Ruth's head. She remembered a familiar pressure of a warm small body pressing against her, tiny hands patting her. "Mommy! I am scared. Mommy, stop them." Terror crept into the voice. Ruth woke with a start. Her heart racing and her chest heaving as if she ran faster than her normal routine. She looked around in a panic and saw she was still in the room assigned to her, in the enormous bed. White sheets glowed faintly in the dark room. Ruth took several deep breaths; her intent was to bring her heart rate down before digi-medic detected the elevated heart rate and the compound medical staff would appear at the door to sedate her.

Ruth got out of the bed, the sheets and blankets tangled in her limbs. She pulled them straight across the bed and walked to the bathroom sink to get a glass of water. A few more deep breaths. The dream still haunted her. Think of something, she cajoled herself and then tried hard to visualize the ocean. Hard, dark sand carved into thousands of ripples by the waves crashing back and forth. The pale blue water with frothing white caps. The silhouettes of the seagulls hovering over screaming in the wind. She focused her mind, imagining the sound of waves gently crashing in and out, in and out. She returned to bed and tried to will herself back to sleep. Thoughts, though, evaded and seeped in, reminding her of whom she used to be.

Molly, her name was Molly. I will never forget you or your father. Ruth's hand moved to the slight bump above her pelvis and traced the ancient scar. It was a thick line about three centimetres and the only physical reminder Ruth had of Molly and being her mother. Ruth heard once in her previous life that the cells in the body completely replace themselves every eighty days — or seven to ten years; probably just bunk, but over the passage of time, her body was remade multiple times over and over and her body still recalled her previous life. The scars of her former life, before she was halted, faded, leaving only faint traces, but the past pains still echoed, even in this small c-section scar.

Ruth felt her stomach. In the recent decades, it was flat and firm as her abdominal muscles pronounced from running and swimming — except that scar. She could remember the swell of her pregnant body, the skin stretched tight over the impossibly enormous belly. She remembered the joy and strangeness of sensation; the baby inside her kicked and turned against her hand. The father, Marco, shared this joy too. He rested his hand gently on her belly and marvelled at her. Billions of babies born into the world, but it still felt like a miracle, like magic. Her mind recalled laying in their bed, second hand and kind of shabby, squeaking at any movement. His body leaned against her back and his hand firmly placed on the swell of her belly. His breathing gradually slowed down, and he inhaled and exhaled deeper and louder as he felt asleep. She always marvelled at the peace and the safety in their shared bed. She recalled vividly how her consciousness slipped into a quiet sleep beside Marco. With this memory, Ruth gradually fell back to sleep. Her mind shut out the reality of the present. In the present, there was no Marco, no Molly. They were now only ghosts she visited in the night's quiet between waking and dreaming.

Chapter 3

Ruth spent the next days preparing herself mentally for Alan's arrival. Shipping boxes arrived daily, brought in by his private helicopter fleet. The boxes contained Alan's clothing and the household effects he required during his trip. Staff, others and morts alike, also returned in small groups to the compound ahead of his arrival.

Melissa and Roger Mahon, the other assistant, argued frequently as they moved about the compound. The compound staff moved frantically about, receiving contradictory orders from Melissa and Roger.

Work started on the ballroom and the grounds. Entertainment was planned and booked; several stages were constructed around the ballroom and garden to spotlight the entertainers and music bands. The entertainers were all morts, selected at any early age and trained in speciality schools. Acrobatics was the latest rage now. Last year's elaborate animal acts were on the wane. The others also craved child acts. These acts never lost popularity. Children were a rarity in the halted world. To see a small child dance and sing was mesmerizing, even to the halted who seemed completely devoid of any trace of humanity.

Alan Blackmore and the rest of his entourage arrived on the Saturday as Melissa had said. Melissa and the other assistances greeted him at the helipad. Ruth saw the flight of helicopters arrive at the compound as she finished her run. She slowed to a walk and waited for security to allow her to pass through. The gate guard seemed to stand taller, be on alert. Another guard was arguing with a gardener. The gardener looked Ruth straight in the eye. It was the same man from last week, same stocky build with dark cropped hair. Ruth swore the man winked at her. She took a second glance at this strange man, and he continued to stare at her. Very unusual, she thought, but she kept her face expressionless. The guard gestured for the man to move on. He seemed irate that the gardener was not in a hurry to leave the grounds. The gate guard, upon closing the gate after Ruth, walked over to the guard and the man to investigate the issue. The gardener made motions to suggest his contrition, bowing and nodding towards the two guards. He shifted the weight of his work bag on his shoulder and headed out the gate.

Ruth slipped into the house and ran to her living space. She closed the door behind her quickly, relieved to avoid Alan a little longer. She debated whether she should avoid the supper tonight. Ruth was famished though. She had run a couple of kilometres longer so she could run through a mort children's park. She pretended to tie her shoelace near a garbage receptacle and hurriedly hid her latest pages — excerpts from a geography textbook, including some rudimentary diagrams. Today Ruth did not see anyone at the mort park other than a mort emptying the garbage receptacles and two mort children on the swings. Others have visited the play park before. Mort children, the only children remaining, were a fascination to others. The others sat on benches specially reserved for them, and watch the children play. Ruth had not seen many halted around for weeks, not since the party season began.

Ruth chanced the trip to the park today as she figured people — the others and morts alike — would be distracted by Alan's arrival and the preparations for his party. She had looped around the park and headed to the ocean. She saw from the corner of her eye, an older mort man, stooped and in ragged clothing, grab the papers and quickly hide them in his waistband. The papers could go to the wrong people or be used against her, Ruth knew, this but seeing a mort with her papers lightened her heart and strengthen her resolve to find some way to get out of her captivity and help the morts.

Ruth showered and dressed. Heading down to the great hall, she thought briefly what she would do if the others found her papers. What would Alan do? Would he punish her? Keep her from leaving the compound? She thought it would be hard for most of them to decipher her cursive. No one wrote in cursive for centuries. Ruth had to teach cursive to herself. She doubted the morts, with their sub par education system, were exposed to cursive so Ruth left a cursive primer in the past, similar to the exercise sheets her grade four teacher gave the class to occupy the students like Ruth who had finished their work well before the rest of the class. This primer was a sort of Rosetta stone.

If an other found her papers, would they gleam her intent? Though it was not outright illegal to communicate to the morts or provide some kind of help, or as she hoped, educate the morts outside the prescribed schools created for them, the others collectively knew an educated mort community was dangerous to their world. It could arm the morts. The others, through increasingly restrictive regulations and laws over the centuries, designed the global community to deprive morts of information that would upset the current order.

Ruth had been copying down texts for several decades now. In the early years, she was full of terror for days after one of her drops, but no one appeared to notice or care. The others in the compound made light of this little hobby of copying books and texts in her room for hours, but they quickly found it dull, just as they found Ruth dull and uninteresting. They could have searched her rooms and found the boxes and boxes of transcribed texts. She thought it best to hide the most of texts in plain sight, keeping a collective of her transcribed papers in her room while bringing the certain parts of her work with her on her run or on whatever excursion she made outside the compound. Ruth tried to vary the topics, hiding technical information amongst literature and history. She knew literature and history were not valued by the others and if those were found, the punishment may be less severe.

Like her running, Ruth grew highly proficient in cursive and could copy out tens of pages in a day. She once read in one of the books and texts stored in her data pad — that a medieval monk took about a year to copy a text on velum which was made from animal skins. Velum was difficult to write on. Its leathery surface absorbed a lot of ink. It took time and considerable effort to form the letters on its surface. Creating sheets of velum in the first place was time consuming, as it took months to stretch and press the velum sheet into pages. Ruth would shame any medieval copyist with the speed with which she put her pen to paper — swift strikes of the pen on smooth sheets of white paper.

The great hall was crowded today with all of Alan's staff assembled back at Blackmore Compound. Ruth was pushed out of the halted area because of the volume of others, so she had to sit in the mort area. She purposely timed her arrival near the end of the dinner service, hoping to avoid Alan. She ate with her head down, her ears on alert for snippets of information. The noise level on both sides was loud and excited. The talk was mostly about the party preparations. In hushed voices, though, Ruth could make out news about conflicts in the east, a failed raid on a halted compound near old New York by a group of morts and then the subsequent retaliation on the surrounding mort settlements.

Ruth's acute hearing isolated Alan's voice. She hated the smug casual drawl he used as he held court with everyone tripping over themselves to please him. Ruth listened as Alan grilled Melissa on the preparations for the party. He interrupted Melissa at least twice to make changes.

"Yes, sir." Melissa replied each time in a deferential tone.

Ruth hurriedly ate, wanting to leave the hall before Alan noticed her. As she rose from the chair, she noticed one of the morts watching her. It looked like the gardener at the gate today, except he was dressed in the house uniform. *What was he doing in here?* Normally the grounds staff departed before the supper hours to their mort settlements. Most of the morts that worked here lived in the mort area of Richmond.

As Ruth left the room, she felt his eyes follow her. A sensation hit her in the gut, like something dropped through her body. She made no movements to show that she noticed him or his attention. As she walked by the dining room, she kept her gaze forward. Out of the corner of her eyes, she saw the gardener on one side and Alan on the other. She was unsettled that Alan too was watching her. She paced her room that night before she retired to her bed, trying to distract herself. It never helped her to overthink.

Ruth, Ruthie, Babe. Are you still working? Come to bed, baby. Ruth dreamt of the old familiar one, when she and Marco shared the tiny bachelor apartment. She had just graduated and started working for LIFETECH in the administration cell. During the first months, she spent evenings creating work lists and researching the company and its projects. She so wanted to do a good job. The pay was crap, but she hoped she could impress the right person and get a better paying position. Marco worked two jobs: bartending and the parts department at an automobile repair shop. His degree was in Labour relations and hers in business, specializing in technology administration. She had started a degree in English literature but changed it in hopes of a better paying career. Marco though stuck to his passion in history and poli-sciences, beyond all reasonable hope. He had no prospects in these fields. Inflation was rapidly rising, and the world seemed to be heading towards increased conflict and environmental disasters. The European Union was threatening to dissolve, and Canada was pressured to join the North America Union with the United States and its hapless partner, Mexico. There was no future for Marco's idealism. Ruth and Marco's life together was a struggle of bills and student loans amidst a world recession to rival all, but they held on to a small ray of hope.

Ruthie, Ruthie. She laughed and jumped into his arms, pulling the blankets over them. She hated that nickname. It sounded like the name of an old lady or spinster aunt. Marco knew it and, as such, used it often to get her attention. *Ruthie.* She loved, however, the sound of his warm, confident voice. Even in her dreams, she constantly worried she will forget his face — squarish, thick eyebrows arching up, the shaggy hair hanging over his eyes which he unconsciously brushes away. Her body ached to feel the warm pressure of his body against her. In the rare, wonderful dreams, she felt him beside her and heard his voice crystal clear, like he was there in the present, in her room. But frequently, the dreams turned dark like tonight. The dream shifted and Ruth watched a reel on repeat — Marco collapsing to the hard floor; his face bloodied and bruised, dead eyes open and unseeing. She screamed over and over. *Marco, Marco!*

Sunday was a day of rest for Ruth. She learnt decades ago that she could only push her body so far with the running and swimming. Despite the high level of care digi-medic and the compound medical team could offer, she was only human — well close enough to human — and susceptible to injury. She allowed herself to sleep in. Sometimes she attempted to draw or paint. In her past life, she enjoyed art and was a decent painter. Her sketches of people were her forte. Now she struggled. Something about the halting took creativity away from her and the others. She still worked at it. She currently was working on a landscape, the ocean view from her runs. Ruth had completed several similar paintings, but something was off, stilted. The act of drawing and painting though distracted her, and she had the time to experience with mixing of colours and varying techniques. The result was always disappointing, but she appreciated the diversion.

Before preparing the paint and paintbrushes, Ruth flipped through her latest sketchbook. There were hundreds of attempts to sketch Marco and Molly. The best pieces she created were those that came the closest to resembling them and she took those pages from the sketch book and framed them. She managed to get the frames from Melissa in a rare moment of kindness.

Now the framed sketches sat on her nightstand. The one picture was of Marco, just his face. It was wrong somehow; she didn't get the angle of his eyebrows right and the lips look clownish. Molly's image, too, was incorrect. Ruth couldn't replicate the curve of the cheeks or the wide bright eyes. She had to settle with what the sketches represented, a memorial of sort. A reminder of who she was and what she lost.

Chapter 4

On the day of the party, Melissa appeared at Ruth's door. She walked in without invitation. Ruth had no autonomy here. She had fewer rights than the average mort. The morts at the end of their workday went to a home and their loved ones. Ruth envied the morts, even more than the others. The others in this compound do not have full autonomy either; they answered to Alan Blackmore and implicitly understood they must keep him happy. This was a familiar arrangement in the halted communities — small oligarchies across the globe with people like Alan Blackmore on top.

"Hello Melissa. Is the party planning going well?" Ruth stood aside near her bed as Melissa walked around, touching Ruth's paintings, the sketchbooks, the boxes. Ruth half expected Melissa to open every drawer and cabinet and to look under the bed and desk.

"Everything looks to be proceeding accordingly," Melissa frowned. Ruth assumed Melissa was stressed. Alan likely made a lot of last minute changes, which was very was typical of Alan. Most of the household appeared to be on edge. Ruth had seen this before.

Ruth then noticed that Melissa was holding a garment bag. It was meant for Ruth, she knew it. Alan Blackmore wanted to dress her up and display her like some obedient dog. He had done this numerous of times in the past. Ruth took the bag and placed it on a reading chair. Melissa's face betrayed her curiosity. She wanted to know more about Ruth and the strange arrangement between Alan and Ruth. Melissa knew, however, the unspoken rule — no one in the compound spoke of Ruth.

Ruth ignored Melissa's pointed glances. She wanted to talk to Melissa, to converse with another person, but she did not trust the younger woman; Melissa was too greedy for status. She would easily betray Ruth or anyone, in fact, for better standing with Alan and his company. She had abandoned her old mort family completely fifty years ago to join the halted on the Blackmore compound. Still, Ruth was profoundly lonely. She wanted to reach out to the younger woman and ask her if she regretted the halt, ask Melissa what it was like as a child in this new world order created by the halt. She wondered often what Melissa's family was like. Instead, Ruth stood there frozen. The two women faced each other, scanning for hidden signs. Ruth was in her drab outfit, the usual long sleeve top and slacks which were purposely dull to avoid attention. Melissa, on the other hand, was in garish blues and greens like a peacock wearing incredibility high, high heels. The outfit demanded attention. Ruth searched for humanity in Melissa's eyes; the younger woman's eyes were heavily decorated with eye liner and glittery powders. Guarded,

Melissa was not budging and offered nothing. Ruth responded in kind.

When Melissa departed, Ruth opened the garment bag. It was an old fashion blazer and pant suit, dark grey with a modest collared shirt in a pale pink. Black flats were at the bottom of the bag. No surprise, Alan had chosen this outfit before. It was the outfit she wore over two hundred years ago, two hundred and fifty years, to be more precise. Not the exact outfit, but a copy; the original was torn and bloodied that day. This one, on the hanger, was like three outfits Ruth wore daily when she worked for Alan Blackmore and LIFETECH all those centuries ago. He never noticed her limited range in office wear back then; he never noticed Ruth, not until that day, the day she and Marco were found out, the day of the fire. *Alan still wants to play this game.* Ruth sighed. She would wear it. Ruth did not want to antagonize him; she wanted to maintain his current level of trust or at least avoid his attention. She wanted to continue her project for as long as she could.

Evening arrived, and the party was in full swing. Guests crowded the ballroom and the grounds to which the ballroom opened out to. Music spilled out from every corner from the mort musicians dressed in sombre suits. They play with stoney faces which contradicted the lively music. Entertainers were stationed throughout the room and grounds — contortionists, gymnasts. A flying trapeze stood in the centre of the grounds. The effect was a frenetic circus dressed in glittery, colourful body suits. Groups of the halted gathered in clusters throughout the party. Most ignored the colourful feats of acrobats and the beautiful melodies as the others had brought their own entertainments. The halted guests dressed as outlandish as possible to impress each other, but even that did not truly interest them. At these events, Ruth always thought of

Marco and his nightly lectures to her in their cramped apartment.

"It's the theory of the leisure class on steroids, Ruth. Bread and circuses! Flaunting their wealth. They sold whatever was left of their pathetic souls and they are selling off all of us and the planet for their vanity."

Ruth walked behind Alan Blackmore and his entourage. There was a pecking order of sorts; first Alan, then Rob and Maury, representing the original halted ones. Melissa followed behind with three other assistants, one of them being Roger. These four were more recently halted. Ruth completed the group, following behind, dull and drab in a version of her old work suit, hundreds of years out of style, if it ever was in fashion.

Alan was in dazzling white silk—pants, shirt, and a small cap tilted on his head. It was almost impossible to source silk, as that industry was in jeopardy prior to the halting began. A disease nearly wiped out the silkworms, as well as other insects such as many species of bees and butterflies. Ruth had to admit the effect of the blinding white made Alan stand out in a crowd of outrageous extravagance. It softened his hard, ferret like features.

Rob and Maury wore richly coloured suits, immaculately tailored. Melissa and the other female assistants competed in elaborate gowns, with plunging necklines and bare backs, asymmetric and again ridiculous shoes. Most of the party, male and female, strategically applied makeup to ensure they stood out. Melissa's expert application highlighted her heart-shaped doll face. Even Ruth relented from her own apathy and applied a little eyeliner and lipstick.

The entourage meandered around the party, pausing often to greet guests. One woman, Bethany Roberts, dressed in a golden yellow robe trimmed with fur. Two mort children, aged about ten years old, carried the train of her dress. Ruth cringed; the sight was a punch to her gut. The children, dressed in matching outfits, conducted their task with the utmost seriousness. Fear showed in their eyes. Bethany Roberts was an original halted and held a position on the company's board of directors. She rivaled Alan Blackmore in importance with LIFETECH and the Council.

Another board member, an older male named Logan Ryan, halted in his fifties, had two mort women, barely out of their teens, by his side. The mort women were near identical, likely siblings. They stood awkwardly beside the man; their arms crossed over their bare midriffs as they shifted frequently in the high heels that the women seemed quite unaccustomed to.

It was common for others to have mort companions or pets. Few within the halted communities maintained close relations other than business partners and colleagues.

Friendships were often strained and broken after a period of time. Most marriages amongst themselves were severed after a couple of decades. Ruth saw many halted couple together, then separate to form relations with others in the halted community. After a couple of centuries, most of the others had dated each other. Many married in spectacular ceremonies and then divorced each other. There was a lot of animosity as a result of the couplings and un-couplings. Very few of the halted could move amicably beyond the failed love matches. The only glue that held the halted community together was their knowledge that they needed each other to uphold their status and to remain on top. No one spoke of their fear of living like the morts but it was presence everywhere.

Ruth expected that part of the failures in the couplings had to do with the fact that the halted, including herself, found themselves sterile. There appeared to be no medical reason to explain why the others could not have children after the halting. A lot of effort in research and development was still focused on solving this issue. LIFETECH had many research projects in this area. There also were no children after coupling with morts or using IVF with mort hosts. Some of the others, desperate to be parents, adopted mort children. Often, they bought mort babies from desperate mort mothers or from mort baby farms, an industry that quickly developed to meet the needs of the halted. Some of the children were halted after they reached adulthood. Some of the others in the room now were once those mort children, but they were hard to identify as they too played the game and were costumed outlandishly to outdo each other.

Ruth stayed in her place behind Alan and his entourage. Others observed her with some interest. Most knew of her history in the household. The newer halted, not privy to the full history, outright gawked, especially at seeing her in her drab outfit. She was dressed like a mort but yet she glowed with health. The freshness of her face and her smooth, clean hands clearly marked her as other, as halted. *It's her*, Ruth heard someone whisper when she passed by. She thought she heard the words, *the fire*.

Ruth had taken a few glasses of wine from the mort waiters over the course of the evening. She planned to get through this evening with a numbing buzz; nothing too much that would make her completely vulnerable. This evening, the whole garish spectacle, was an insult to her eyes and ears. She made some important observations about the shifting alliances though. Bethany Roberts and Alan Blackmore were clearly on the outs. Rumour was that Bethany Roberts was talking behind Alan's back in the shadows, trying to gain influence with the board and dismantle Alan's dominance. Walter Baldwin, of Dynalife Industries, was holding court in the ballroom — his voice overly loud mingled with forced laughter. His company was Alan's biggest competitor in the Americas. Alan had spoken in ear shot of Ruth to Maury that he expected Dynalife was behind the mort strikes in the interior, attempting to destabilize LIFETECH.

The night carried on and on. Ruth wanted badly to leave. She had to wait for Melissa to give the okay. Ruth noticed that Alan had had a lot to drink, and she feared he would punish her in front of the group if she attempted to leave or if she brought too much attention onto herself. It had happened a century ago. Fueled by alcohol, Alan screamed and screamed at her, slapping her until he grew tired. That was a rare moment in which he let himself lose control in front of people outside the Blackmore compound. Tonight, though, she would not chance his temper, so she was forced to be in this madhouse of a party until she got the sign.

Her eyes, heavy and sore, started to blur with the dramatic movement of the entertainers' colourful bodies and the visual assault that was the colourful oddity of the others preening before each other in every hue and texture. Her back ached from standing. Meanwhile, the music, competing from all the corners, poured obnoxiously into her ears; Ruth's head throbbed murderously.

"Ruth, good to see you," a male voice murmured, and she turned to see it was Anthony. Anthony Gelinas, a handsome male who appeared to be in his mid forties, was on the board of directors at LIFETECH. He was also Ruth's former lover. Ruth met Anthony in the early decades after the halting. Back then, the others were not yet tired of each other and spent much more time together, and the parties lasted for weeks. And then there were the excursions — the pyramids in Egypt, the Great Wall of China, the Swiss Alps. The halted community travelled the world together, seeking thrills and novelty until they all grew tired and jaded.

Ruth was dragged out to all of it — Alan's trophy, the last of the rebels. She had recovered from her serious life-threatening injuries and was beginning to come out of the deep medicated depression. Anthony took an interest in her and persuaded Alan to let him woo her. Ruth expected Anthony paid Alan somehow, maybe gave Alan some of his shares, which would have allowed Alan to have more control of LIFETECH. Why else would Alan let Ruth leave the compound? He had seemed so determined to punish her under his watch.

At first, Ruth tried to avoid Anthony, but he was persistent. He politely inquired about her and sought opportunities to make small talk. Ruth also learnt that Anthony was very intelligent. He could hold conversations about a variety of subjects, such as history, literature and philosophy. He had a pragmatic view on things and Ruth began to enjoy their discussions, despite that he was one of them. One day, Anthony invited her to travel to the Polynesian islands with him on his yacht — all the affluent others had yachts, as well as private aircraft. Despite herself, she agreed to go. Ruth hated herself for wanting to be with him, but she was profoundly lonely. She assumed she was being used as a diversion or a plaything, but she needed her own diversion. She wondered if Marco would ever understand why she went and if he would forgive her. Marco was very black and white on things, unyielding in upholding a high standard of principles.

That initial trip extended into other trips and then Ruth had fully moved in with Anthony. All in all, Ruth stayed with Anthony for nearly ninety years.

"Hello Anthony. Are you well?" she asked, but she barely listened to his response; she was concerned Alan would notice the two of them talking. Alan, however, was preoccupied with other guests. Ruth looked closer at Anthony; he was handsome and knew it. Though dressed well, he kept his outfit subtle, tasteful and understated. Anthony reminded her of Marco in the set of his eyes; he was a similar built too. Both men were highly intelligent, but Anthony lacked Marco's passionate nature and firm sense of morality.

"I am well," Ruth automatically replied when she realized Anthony had asked about her wellbeing and was waiting for a response. She found it strange to resort to old conventions of polite conversation. The words hung in the air, incongruous with the reality. She was a quasi captive; he, an old lover, was a part of LIFETECH. Ruth almost destroyed LIFETECH and the halt that day of the fire, and Anthony was the one fifth of LIFETECH.

Ruth saw Alan had finally noticed Anthony and was watching the two with a small frown. He clearly did not approve of the two and the remnants of their relationship. Ruth was unsure of what Anthony got from their eight decades of being together. For Ruth, the relationship was a long reprieve from Alan's compound and constant monitoring. She did come to care for Anthony and appreciate his company, but their relationship had limits. She could not fully trust Anthony with her thoughts. He appeared as two people. With her, he was a normal person, like someone from before the halt. They did the typical couple things — well, wealthy couple things — such as spending time together in luxurious settings, most of which were his various properties around the world. Over the decades, they settled comfortably in a mutually satisfying silence. They enjoyed fine food and explored the natural wonders of the world. When they conversed, it was about prehalt times, normally of philosophy and art, sometimes history. Nothing ever too political or controversial. It was like a long honeymoon or holiday. Hundreds of moments, they came together; bodies craving affection and intimacy.

It was inevitable, though, that Anthony would grow bored after decades. Ruth saw no real substance in their time together. They had over familiarity of each other's bodies but not of their hearts. Ruth then found herself back in her gilded cage at the Blackmore compound. Alan had looked at her with a smug "I knew it would end" look for several months.

Anthony, noticing Alan, nodded calmly in his direction. Ruth wondered, not for the first time, what Anthony had over Alan; Alan always has a stifled, angry look in Anthony's presence. Then Anthony looked into Ruth's face. His hand caressed her cheek with a tentative show of affection, an old familiar gesture that caught Ruth off guard. He wanted to say something to her. She raised an eyebrow, a silent question to him, but he moved away from her and Alan's entourage.

The group was outside now. The sun had set three hours ago, but it was still warm. Ruth felt better because of the fresh air. The grounds were not as crowded, the music not as in her face. She allowed herself to an escape as she relived in her head an old favourite memory — a visit to the beach with Marco and Molly. Molly was almost three; Ruth recalled adorably chubby arms and legs in constant motion. Molly screamed with delight as the waves moved over her chubby bare feet. Marco stooped next to Molly, holding her hand protectively.

Her reverie was interrupted when she detected a shift in the mood in the entourage. Alan seemed to grow tense suddenly, and of course the others grew agitated. Allan abruptly dismissed everyone and walked to a group at the far edge of the grounds. It stood the core board of directors

— Bethany Roberts, Logan Ryan, and Anthony. Judging by their stoney expressions, they clearly had some urgent business to discuss. Ruth could not gage anything other than it must be very serious, as the board members were all solemn. Around her, the party was at full swing; many were now extremely drunk and loud.

Ruth cautiously moved back inside the ballroom. She intended to leave immediately for the sanctuary of her room while no one was paying any attention. Melissa and the others used the opportunity to scatter and mingle with people of their choosing–as well as topping up their drinks. A waiter brushed by her, bumping her elbow. It was the gardener from the gate. What was he doing in wait staff attire? The look on his face suggested he purposely bumped her elbow. He practically winked at her. She nearly gasped. Ruth looked to see if anyone was observing her, but the crowd seemed absorbed in their own worlds, extremely inebriated. Ruth continued towards the doors, trying not to increase her pace visually and draw attention to herself. She walked up the hall outside the ballroom and headed to the lift.

"Wait. Wait." It was him, the gardener, now dressed wait staff in black and white. His face was flushed from moving quickly. Instinctively, both darted their eyes around them to confirm if they were alone. No one else was in the hall; they faced each other. The man stood about three inches taller and had a stocky, muscular build. His face was brown and weathered from the sun. Overall, he appeared to be about early thirties, similar to Ruth's own age, before she was halted. Ruth waited for him to speak.

"We have been collecting your papers. The ones you leave around the mort settlement," he stated.

Ruth did not reply, so he continued, "We want to discuss access to some particular texts."

"Who are you talking about?" she finally braved a question. The man before her did not seem threatening. His tone was sincere, appealing to her for help with earnest. Could she trust him?

"Some of us in the settlements want a better life for our children. The corporations are planning to limit our schools and education further. Those papers. You want to help us, don't you? Why else are you providing them? You are Ruth Anderson, Ruth Guzman? The one who sabotaged LIFETECH in the great fire?"

"Who are you?" Ruth avoided his questions. She stared at the man, his face open and earnest — a departure from the closed, untrusting Blackmore household. Ruth immediately wanted to trust this man. She was so damn lonely, so tired of being alone. She needed to trust someone, and she felt a reckless urge to trust this man.

"Paul Foster. My family has lived in this area for centuries; most of us are in Richmond. The community has been collecting your papers for decades. We have used them in the schools for decades."

Ruth was stunned. She wanted to cry or laugh, but she was afraid to react. All this time she wondered if they found her work, if they realized what it was, and now to have confirmed that the papers were in the morts' hands; it was surreal.

Laughter rang out from down the hall. People were coming, the others. Morts would not dare to be so bold and carefree, to be loud and free in their actions.

"I have to go." Ruth turned to the lift, dreading to be seen with this mort man called Paul. It was dangerous for both of them.

"Please, I will try to contact you later. On one of your runs." His eyes pleaded with her. She quickly entered the lift when the lift door opened. She stood to face him again, too terrified to reply.

In the safety of her room, Ruth paced. She wanted the papers to be found by the morts, but she was still terrified. *They got them; they got the papers.* She saw on several occasions that morts picked up her papers, but she did not know if they knew what the papers were.

She visualized Paul's face — human, not like the typical halted which often was tucked and tugged, and pale from lack of exposure to the elements. The same questions played over and over in her head. *Who else saw them? Can they read them? What if Alan or any of the others find out?* The Corporations have steadily taken control of the global nations after cyber wars destroyed most of the G7 governments. Morts sequentially have had their rights systemically stripped as they were corralled into settlements and ghettos. They were allowed to continue attending schools, but the curriculums just offered the basics; school was more of a holding place for mort children until they joined the work force. Schools were essentially a daycare while the mort adults worked all day.

Imagining Molly attending these schools bothered Ruth. Molly must have attended one, Ruth reasoned. After the fire at LIFETECH — Marco was dead and Ruth was in intensive care for almost a year — Molly was lost to her. Ruth suspected Marco's family took Molly with them and went into hiding. They probably changed Molly's name. Hundreds of years later, the idea that Molly would have been denied an education just like the other morts nagged at Ruth. Molly would have been denied a future — forced into a settlement, and subsequently confined to that settlement for the rest of her life. Poor medical care and limited education. Molly would have had few options for employment, probably housekeeping or factory work. Maybe she was forced to serve in the Council militia. Or maybe Molly was part of the morts that lived feral, outside the settlements, in the ruins of the cities, or in far reaches of the remaining wilderness. Ruth shuddered at that thought; she heard that life in the ruins of the cities was brutal and violent. Outside the settlements, morts were more vulnerable.

Ruth's transcriptions of books and texts were her rebellion against LIFETECH and Alan Blackmore. She took a datapad from Anthony; the idea germinating in her mind even back then. She waited for several years to pass, after Anthony returned her to the Blackmore compound, and then began her work. Her mother had taught her cursive long ago, digging up ancient school workbooks. Ruth used those workbooks often when she played school with the neighbour's girl.

That night, Ruth dreamt of the fire. Ruth and Marco are caught in the server room. They snuck in that evening using Ruth's access card. They left Molly earlier that evening with Marco's brother, Michael, as a precaution. After months of planning, it was finally happening. They were hitting LIFETECH. Another group hit Dynalife last month. Ruth didn't know many details and that was the point; the groups kept the resistant cells in the dark about the other cells for operation security. Ruth's role was to get them — Marco and the three others in the cell — into LIFETECH and the server rooms. It seemed to go smoothly. They entered the building after eleven pm as planned, bypassing the security guards after months of studying the guard rotation. Ruth and Marco were tasked with server room two. Ruth was almost giddy with the adventure, sneaking past the front security, using the access cards Ruth stole weeks ago. She had spent over a month worrying herself nearly sick — her stomach was a mess, and she could hardly eat — after she agreed to help. Now she almost felt gleeful relief after they successfully snuck past the guards.

Marco and Ruth entered their assigned server room. As the door closed, Marco turned to her and kissed her passionately.

"We do this for Molly, eh? We stop the stranglehold for Molly and her generation. Fuck those guys. Fucking tech overlords." Marco whispered fiercely. Ruth nodded; she was not as absolute, so certain in her convictions, as Marco. She had to be coaxed to join the resistance. Ruth though wanted to do something, so Molly had a chance of some quality of life. Helping Marco with this seemed like her best opportunity.

They went to work. Marco was to upload the virus the resistance created. The others were in server room one, with the same task. They assigned Ruth to keep watch, so she opened the door again, just enough to peer down the hallway. She also had the burner phone to set off the explosives as Plan B. Oh god, could she even go through with Plan B? She placed the explosives near the centre of the server and prepped the charger just as she rehearsed with Marco. Its number was listed on the burner phone as a contact, ready to dial. Ruth waited as Marco attached the hard drive to the server's main frame. The upload started, 5%, 12%. Time seemed to have slowed down and the tension was building. All they had to do was to ensure the upload was complete and then they could depart. Ruth was not even sure what the virus would do. *Stop it all*, she hoped. *Stop LIFETECH's stupid plan to live forever.* Somehow, LIFETECH was winning the immortality race and found the way to halt aging. It was clear, even to Ruth, that only a few would reap the benefit — Alan for certain and his lackeys, Silicon Valley North group, the tech corporations across the globe. *Damn greedy bastards.* They will stomp all over people, ordinary people like Ruth and Marco. Molly needed a chance to escape the poverty Ruth saw their little family sink into deeper each year. Ruth had to agree with Marco on this. She finally opened her eyes and saw firsthand how ruthless LIFETECH and Alan Blackmore were.

It was a report Ruth read last month that finally persuaded her to join Marco's group. Ruth had not seen a report like this one, so she suspected it was accidentally given to her when she was told to make copies of documents for the upcoming board meeting. She opened it to separate the pages and there it was, entitled Age-halting Breakthrough. In it, Marco's claims were apparently very real. LIFETECH discovered the process to halt aging after several trials on animals and 'human' test subjects, in which most subjects died. Even Ruth could read between the lines in the report which mentioned morbidity percentages. The report was more concerned with questions on how to market it to an upscale clientele and how to combat negative scrutiny regarding the unauthorized trials and its casualties. Those who died in the process were just numbers hidden in tables and annexes.

Ruth snuck out a copy of the report to give to Marco and his group. The contents incensed but did not surprise them. One of the group members heard rumours of how bodies used in the trials were dumped in a local landfill.

"They got the city officials on the take. Lets them do what they want. Homeless doesn't matter to the city, anyway. They are just a nuisance."

78% uploaded. They heard a ruckus in the hall. *Is it from the other server room? Hurry up,* Ruth willed the hard drive. She could barely look at Marcus; it was too much for her, too dangerous. Her heart was pounding in her chest; she felt sicken, lightheaded.

"Stop! Lay down!" Two armed security guards broke through the door. Alan Blackmore was behind them with Maury Poirrier.

"Get down! Get down!"

Marco grabbed at one of the security guards. Their two bodies collided with the electronic equipment, processors, and servers. Ruth heard the two grunting. Ruth was screaming now. She heard gunshots. Marco collapsed. The guards moved in on his prone body, kicking and stomping.

"Marco! Stop it! Stop it!" Ruth screamed, and a guard moved towards her, swinging a baton. The first hit was across her jaw. Then the blows hit her all over, up and down her body. She could not defend herself or help

Marco. She dropped into a fetal position against the wall, seeing Marco on the ground beside her, crumbled and still. Blood was everywhere. She tried to reach out to him. A faceless guard stomped on her shoulder and arm over and over. He kicked her repeatedly, making contact with her back and hips. The pain was intense, shooting throughout. Alan's face hovered above them, pale and alien.

"Marco. Marco." Ruth whimpered and then everything went black.

Chapter 5

Ruth had been working at LIFETECH for over a year when she found out she was pregnant. It was not planned; she cried as the blue strip appeared on the pregnancy test. She was only 24 years old, and they had so much student debt. It seemed like they would never pay off their loans. Marco was still struggling to find a good paying job. Unemployment was high, inflation out of control, and the world seemed crazy with conflict and erratic weather. How could they support a baby? How could they bring a baby into such a world? The future was so uncertain and unstable.

Marco came home from work that night to find Ruth sitting hunched on the living room couch in the dark, hugging her knees. She hadn't moved for hours since she took the test. It was like he knew; he immediately sat beside her and put his arm around her. She sobbed as she showed him the offending test. It was a while before either of them spoke.

"Ruthie, it will be okay. Baby, don't cry. We are in this together." Marco finally broke the silence.

There was no talk of abortion or giving away the baby. One of those actions would have been the logical decision. The recently elected government just reduced parental leave to six months and LIFETECH was notorious for allowing the bare basics for benefits. Ruth heard last year that a woman lost her position when she asked for parental leave. Ruth and Marco were in unison with the decision to keep this baby and raise it. Despite all the upcoming hardships, they were excited. They wanted to be a family eventually, and their love for each other seemed to grow as Ruth's belly grew. The idea of being parents together brought joy and wonder. They would find a way together.

Ruth and Marco also were thankful for Marco's mom, Anna, and their circle of friends. Everyone seemed legitimately happy for them. People, even neighbours they hardly spoke to, smiled at the sight of her growing belly and many brought over small gifts — dishes of food, baby clothes, a well used stroller. Older women in their apartment tried to touch her growing belly and gave advice. "Avoid coffee and chocolate." "Sleep while you can." The superintendent, when first hearing their news, broke out in a huge grin. Ruth saw that the prospect of a baby brought hope to them all and rallied their circle into a tighter knit community. And the circle grew to include the residents at the apartment, the locals in the shops Ruth frequented, and all their friends and family. Clearly, people in the neighbourhood, and in their lives, were attracted to the idea of a baby. A baby gave hope.

Ruth soon found herself five months pregnant. The time went by fast. So far, there were only minor issues at work once she got over the brief period of nausea. One Tuesday, she was busy preparing for an upcoming shareholders' meeting. She kept finding small typos in the quarterly report, causing her to move back and forth to her desk, the printer, and the shredding machine. *Was this pregnancy brain?* Her coworkers teased her often about pregnancy brain and Ruth would laugh with them, though sometimes it was a touch irritating.

After the third trip to the shredder, Ruth paused to grab a snack. A handful of trail mix helped her through these months, with the nausea and the low energy. She then walked to the washroom to clean up. Lost in thought, she did not notice the boss was in the hallway — Alan Blackmore. She rarely saw him, especially on the admin floor. She nearly bumped against him.

"Afternoon sir." She recovered, wiping her damp hands on the sides of her legs. She then smoothed her top, which was inching up over her belly. His eyes darted there, at her round belly, and then at her face; acknowledging her for likely the first time since she started her employment at LIFETECH. He frowned. Ruth had the feeling her pregnancy and upcoming parental leave was a nasty inconvenience to him and most of LIFETECH. Only her section in admin and two of the friendlier security staff guards acknowledged her situation with good humour.

Alan Blackmore then changed his look of disapproval to an insincere smile.

"Do you know where Janice is?" he asked impatiently. She apologized as she had not seen Janice since morning. Janice Rogers was the Chief HR. He briskly moved past Ruth. Alan Blackmore, she recalled, was one of the original founders of LIFETECH. He had a reputation of his maverick, bold ideas. Some say he was a genius; others a pompous ass who used people up. Marco called Alan Blackmore was a sociopath.

Ruth opted to start her parental leave on October first, the week that the doctor predicted the baby would be born. HR was badgering her to choose a date so they can sort out a temp for her. It seemed pushy and insensitive. Babies came when they were ready, the doctor and Marco's mom told her this numerous times. What if something went wrong? What if the baby came early, or she lost it? How would HR deal with that inconvenience? Ruth, however, woke on October second to the sensation of her uterus contracting. It was like a mini earthquake, leaving Ruth a bit more breathless each time.

The contractions were soon five minutes a part and Marco grabbed the go-bag. They splurged on a taxi to the hospital.

They were excited and terrified. Marco's eyes shone bright, and Ruth saw his eyes were damp with tears of excitement.

The taxi ride was torture. A rally occurred near city hall, two blocks away. Ruth heard through the glass window of the taxi protestors screaming. Protect the people! Stop Corporate Takeover! Protect the Social Net! Marco would have been at the rally if not for the baby. He volunteered with a local group that tried to act as a watchdog, sounding out alarms as worker benefits such as Ruth's maternity leave and pensions were being reduced and stripped. Marco, the Labour history expert, was in his glory with this group — fighting against the establishment. Ruth was glad he was not involved in the rally today. Not only did she need him today, but the protests were getting dangerous. Police vehicles were everywhere, including in their neighbourhood. People were bound to get hurt with the clash of the protestors against an angrier counter group, who were screaming how they were filthy communists or lazy parasites.

"LIFETECH pays that mob to be disruptive, Ruth. LIFETECH is evil," Marco argued with Ruth months ago after a rally where Marco was nearly arrested. A huge brawl had broken out between the protestors and the counter protesters — the paid mob, as Marco called them.

"What do you want me to do, Marco? Quit LIFETECH and get two to three jobs that pay a lot less so we can still pay rent? We have a child on the way to think about."

The taxi ride was almost an hour longer than expected because of the roadblocks. Inside the cab, an angry chorus of shouting and rally cries were muffled but still audible. Rationally, Ruth knew she would still be in labour for several more hours. First born babies did not arrive quickly according to all the books and Marco's mother.

Emotionally, though, Ruth was terrified. She did not want

to give birth in the back seat of a cab. She did not want to give birth in such a tumultuous time. Were they doing the right thing — Ruth worried yet again — having a baby when the entire world seemed at war?

In the hospital, Ruth was hooked up to IV and confined to the bed. The nurse said the baby was low in the canal and sitting up or walking were not options. Ruth's plans were to be as mobile as possible, maybe sit on an exercise ball or hang over the birthing bar like a video they watched during the birthing course. Those plans dashed against the rocks. Ruth also wanted to avoid any drugs or interventions. The doctor, who finally showed up five hours after Ruth was admitted, warned her that a C-section might have to happen. Ruth relented and let the anesthesiologist insert the spinal needle. Soon she was being prepped for surgery and Marco's face was pale with worry.

Ruth laid in the surgical room, looking up at the ceiling. Her body, below her armpits to her toes, was numb, alienated from her. Marco stood stoically by her side. She heard the muffled cries of a baby, her baby. She could see nothing except the ceiling, Marco, and the nurse by her other side. A white partition obscured the surgery from her. Marco was now out of view, behind the partition. Ruth heard the doctor offering Marco the opportunity to cut the umbilical cord. Moments later, the doctor presented Ruth with a bundle wrapped in the white and blue hospital flannel. Marco had to help her hold the bundle. It was her baby, a healthy baby girl — round and yellowish head, face scrunched up in anger, and body wrapped tight like an Egyptian mummified cat. Ruth already loved her more than anything in the world and she could tell by Marco's expression that he felt the same way.

Molly, let's call her Molly Anna, Marco had suggested months ago after learning the baby was a girl. Molly was Ruth's mother's name. She had died two years ago of breast cancer. Anna was Marco's mother, alive and well, living a block away. *Oh Marco, yes, that would be perfect.* Molly Anna Guzman was born on the third of October 2031.

Chapter 6

A week after the party and Ruth had heard nothing from Paul, the strange mort man. She resumed her usual routine. The others in the house seemed to be following suit. She rarely saw them except at supper time. Blissfully, Alan Blackmore seemed not to notice her. She wondered if he had a new project or a new mort plaything. She felt a ping of guilt if it was the latter. Her freedom or general wellbeing should not be tied to another person's deprivation.

Her run was routine. She smuggled out this time a complicated text regarding calculus with lots of mathematical equations. It was not her first time transcribing mathematic books, so she had a basic understanding of the concepts. She hid it in the tree trunk at the edge of the wood line, the hiding spot she thought was the safest.

Upon her return, she saw Paul on the grounds, dressed as a gardener. He did not seem to notice her. Perhaps he was avoiding her. Just as well. It would not be safe for him to interact with her. The other morts could tell him that. As Ruth slowed down to walk through the gate, the vehicle gate screeched as it slowly opened. A dark luxury vehicle entered; the windows tinted dark. She continued towards the house until she heard her name. It was Anthony Gelinas, walking from the parked vehicle.

"Ruth, good to see you." His face lit up into a warm, genuine smile. She could not help but return the smile.

"May I walk you to the house?"

Ruth nodded. She wished she could say no — she was apprehensive about what he wanted from her after all this time — but he had the upper hand. She hoped Alan was not on the grounds today to see them together.

"Alan and the others are away at the Richmond headquarters," Anthony reassured Ruth. "I am here to speak with Melissa. I'm quite early, so we have a few moments."

This piqued her interest further. Ruth wondered if Anthony intentionally planned on meeting up with her and the meeting with Melissa was an excuse. *What did he really want?*

"This is a surprise. To see you today." Ruth felt the need to say something. He nodded amicably and instead of heading into the house, he guided her to a shaded patio. It was extremely warm again. Her clothing was completely damp from today's run. They sat facing each other. Anthony motioned for his assistant to get some cold beverages for them.

"How are you keeping yourself?" Antony finally spoke after drinks were served and all others were out of earshot. His personal bodyguard stood twenty meters away, keeping watch. All the important halted had security; Anthony was no exception.

"Fine," Ruth said automatically. She paused and then spoke candidly. "I don't know how to answer that question truthfully. I lost the art of small talk centuries ago and honestly, you know my circumstances better than most." Ruth winched; she sounded rude.

Ruth felt like she could almost trust Anthony, trust him enough to be honest, but she also knew he was holding a lot from her. Somehow, she owed her safety to him. She did not know why he would bother to influence things to keep her safe, but she was here, still alive and relatively left alone in this compound since he left Ruth all those years.

Anthony somehow ensured her safety; she firmly believed that.

"Alan and the others? Are they treating you humanely?"

"They haven't tried to harm me." She replied. Before Anthony had taken an interest in her all those years ago and took her out of the compound, life at Blackmore compound was a nightmare. The others targeted her, playing games, threatening to violate her. A couple of time they — well, she blocked that from her mind. Leaving the Blackmore compound with Anthony stopped that terror, but then he returned her back. She had no obvious answer to what happened for her return, other than he grew bored with her. She should hate this man, treating her like some type of novelty and then discarding her, but she felt relieved back then. Whatever was between them — love, companionship, respite from loneliness — had run its course over the years and Ruth found she wanted to be alone, alone with her thoughts and memories. Some part of her had grown to love Anthony, the part of her she labelled painfully human and needy. Another part of herself wanted to return to mourning for Marco and Molly and her old life. That part hated herself for her feelings for Anthony.

"Oh, Alan should know full well what I will do if he harms you." Anthony's face reveals a mix of guilt and anger. *Then why did you return me here?* She wondered for the millionth time about what was going on with the Board of Directors and specifically Alan Blackmore and Anthony. Why was Ruth a pawn still, after decades and decades?

"Why are you here?" She asked, expecting him to skirt the truth like he always did. He startled her as he grabbed her hand. He was nearly brimming with emotion, which was very unlike the old familiar Anthony.

"Have you heard of the mort resistant? Here, on the coast?"

"I heard attempted sabotage at some sites in the interior. I know there are revolts in the west. Large protests in Europe. Surely you don't think I am involved?" Ruth noticed Alan's security guards remained visible but were out of earshot. She wondered if Anthony knew about her writings. Ruth hoped her writings would help the morts somehow. Knowledge is power, Marco often said, and denying information was control. She daydreamed, as she copied the texts, of mort children sitting in their schools reading from books created by the stolen texts she offered out. She was guilty, she believed, of foolishness. Stolen pages in a tree trunk won't free morts from the control of the others. She didn't think, though, Anthony would see her writings as connected to the mort resistance.

"The morts here are more organized than Alan and the rest of the board give credit to." Anthony looked into Ruth's face, his expression heavy.

"Anthony, I don't know what to say. I am not involved with the morts. You know that. I am hated by them as much as I am hated by Alan and the others. I have no idea why LIFETECH continues to hold me here, other than it pleases Alan to see me imprisoned in his own home."

"I should never have let you go, Ruth. I have regretted that the moment I returned you. But I think I needed the time to really think about my role in the halting. This world we created. It's hollow. We are stalled, stuck in our own trap. We are dead inside."

Ruth was stunned to hear these words from Anthony. Anthony was not one to be retrospective. He had signed on centuries ago to the corporations' plan willingly and with no remorse. Though he was kind and often loving with Ruth, she saw his arrogant confidence. Anthony believed that he, above all others, deserved his place as an immortal.

She felt he always believed he was superior to her and, of course, to the morts, and perhaps most of the halted.

"Ruth, be prepared. I want to get you out of here. I don't expect to resume our old relationship. You probably hate me but I need for you to be safe. I don't know if you could ever forgive me for everything I've done or not done. But please know I want you to be safe. I have been a damn fool. So foolish."

"Why are you saying this? What do you mean?" Was he toying with her? Anthony pressed her hand harder and slipped off his chair to kneel in front of her. She looked frantically around. The Blackmore security patrol was out of sight and Anthony's bodyguard was facing away, his back only visible to Ruth.

Anthony kissed her suddenly, pulling her face to his. He whispered in her ear. "Things are going to change. Keep alert. Avoid Alan."

He then stood up and called out to his bodyguard. They left Ruth sitting in the shade. She found herself shivering.

Chapter 7

August arrived. The heat of the summer was at its peak. Ruth ran towards the woods, relishing the idea of cover from the sun. She heard another drone behind her. Lately, she had encountered a drone nearly every week, several times a week, in fact. Was Alan increasing surveillance on her?

The drone could not follow her into the woods. The dark of the woods gave an illusion of relief from the heat. Ruth lingered at the stream. She felt her running shoes grow damp as she bent over and cupped her hands in the cool running water. She splashed the water across her face, relishing the cold drops over her hot sweaty face. Over the gentle running water of the creek, Ruth heard a sharp sound. Ruth did not recognize it and she shot a long glance around her, ready to bolt. She saw a man standing across the ancient riverbed, above her, in the shadow of the trees. It was Paul Foster, the mort. He beckoned her over, hands splayed open in a gesture of harmlessness.

"It is dangerous to be here in this heat. Plus, if Blackmore security finds you, it won't bode well." Ruth spoke, irritated by the fear caused by Paul's sudden appearance. Paul was sweaty and red from the heat. She took her small water bottle from her waist belt and offered it to the mort man, worried he would fall ill from the heat. He brushed her bottle away and gestured to his backpack under a tree. He came prepared.

"What do you want?" Ruth had no patience; she could not linger too long. Security would notice and alert Alan.

"We have your writings."

But Ruth already knew that.

"How long have the morts collected them?" She was curious to know if they had found most of the ones she left in this area.

"Over thirty years' worth. Give or take. It took a while to decipher your handwriting. I hope you will be pleased to know we copied what we could and distributed them to the other mort settlements."

Ruth broke out into a wide smile, her face hurting from the unfamiliar facial expression. Her eyes felt wet with emotion. She wanted to ask so many questions. *Were the papers welcome? Useful? Can I do more?*

Her display of emotion startled Paul, but he returned the smile.

"Who are you, Ruth? We think we know your name. Ruth Anderson Guzman, is it not? You are the one who blew up LIFETECH?"

Ruth laughed, a small chortle; she has not heard her full name in centuries and to say she blew up LIFETECH was a stretch.

"Well, I was there when the fire happened. There was a group of us. I didn't blow anything up. It was more my spouse and his colleagues than me." She then was silent, remembering Marco, fierce and brave. "His name was Marco Guzman. We had a daughter, Molly, Molly Guzman."

There was a long silence. Both of them were sizing each other up. Could they trust each other?

"Ruth Guzman. There is something you should know. Molly Guzman was my ancestor. My father's mother was a Guzman. I think you are my ancestor."

Ruth's knees buckled; Paul reached out his hand, but she brushed him away. They stared at each other wordlessly.

Ruth looked for signs of familial similarities. His eyes, maybe. They were medium brown with a black rim. Dark eyebrows arched above them, giving a twinkle — like Marco's and Molly's. His height was similar to her own. What were the chances that came from her own genes?

A twig snapped, and they heard the rustling of branches. The trance broke. They both turned to see a fox dart by.

"I should go." Ruth spoke reluctantly. He nodded.

"I will be here again. We should talk more."

"What do you want, exactly? Why contact me now?"

"We need specific texts. I will have a list next time. I also wanted, well, I just had to know if you were really Ruth Anderson Guzman, if we were related, as my grandmother said." Paul spoke as he started to leave, giving her another long look. *What does he see when he looks at me*? Ruth wondered. *Do I remind him of one of his grandparents? An aunt?* Without a farewell, they parted. Ruth increased her usual pace slightly, so she exited the woods close to the expected time.

A couple of days later, they met again at the creek in the shadows of the trees. Paul had the list; she would look at it later in her room. He also had a photograph, ancient and yellowing. An older man and a woman in her thirties. Ruth recognized Marco's brother, Michael, after a few moments. The photo was in rough shape and the images were fading. Then Ruth realized the woman was Molly. Her Molly. Ruth's last image of Molly was one of a six-year-old girl, the night they left her with Marco's brother.

The woman was Ruth's height and built. She had her father's eyes and hair. Her face shape was more oval, like Ruth's. She was smiling in the photography, arms around an aged Micheal.

"Molly Guzman was my grandmother's grandmother." Paul then explained the family connection.

They both survived! Tears pricked at Ruth, hot and stinging. Paul stopped talking, immediately showing concern.

"It is okay. I'm okay. I haven't seen their faces for a long time. I wasn't able to track them down after the fire. I was so afraid something terrible happened. Oh god, Molly. She grew up! She survived!" Ruth wrapped the photo up with the list, a small piece of scrap paper, in a plastic bag and hid them in a pocket.

"It might take a while to find what you want," she cautioned Paul, "But I will try to get it done."

Then he did the strangest thing. He reached out and pulled her into an embrace. In her state, Ruth was reminded of Michael, her brother-in-law. Michael was a gentle soul, like his mother, Anna. *At least I know Molly was cared for. Michael would have loved her as much as Marco and me.* Ruth let herself be held, her tears wetting Paul's shoulder.

Later, in her room, Ruth read the list: books on coding, journals on the science of anti-aging and histories of the halt. If the morts were searching for their own immortality, she would caution them that it was a terrible thing to stop aging, to outlive your child. Living as long as Ruth had done was lonely and monotonous. It killed joy and love. It destroyed meaning.

She stared at the photograph for a very long time until the pain in her neck and shoulder made it unbearable. She then laid the photograph on the desk gently. She did not want to touch it in case the oils from her hands would destroy it. Reluctantly, she hid it in her closet in a shoe box. She picked up Anthony's old datapad and searched for the texts Paul requested. Most of them were easy to find, but it would take several months to transcribe them all. She wondered if she should just give Paul the datapad. It was a risk, though. If law enforcement found the datapad with the morts, Paul and his family would be severely punished. It could be traced back to Anthony and then to herself, labelling them as part of the mort resistance.

The datapad also required electrical power, which many mort homes could not provide; their infrastructure was poor and unreliable. Ruth was uncertain if Paul could recharge it. She would confirm with him if he wanted to risk taking the datapad. Perhaps she could find another datapad; she could steal one from one of the Blackmore halted. Ruth could take bigger risks now, especially now she knew her writings were going to the right people. Now she had a family again to fight for.

Part of Ruth, though, wanted to continue her writings. It gave the meaning and purpose in her life she craved since

Marco's death and it now connected her to family. She then decided; Ruth will transcribe the requested texts and carry on with her work. Perhaps she could do more. She wanted to do so much more.

Chapter 8

Through the months of August and September, Ruth smuggled out over half of the texts on the list. She was dropping off twice and three times her usual activity. The drop offs were now at the creek area. Most of the time, Paul was there waiting. If not, she hid them in the tree where Paul stood the first time they met in the woods.

When Paul was waiting, it was a moment of joy. She questioned him about his family and the mort settlement. She learnt there were many Anderson Guzman descendants in the mort settlement and several who had moved on. Paul estimated he had about sixty cousins, once, twice, or more removed. Paul himself had an older sister. Both of his parents had died recently; both had cancer. Morts rarely lived beyond sixty nowadays. Healthcare available to them was primitive and cancers were prevalent because of exposure to chemicals in their jobs. There was also a profound lack of regard for their overall safety when working for the others and accidents were frequent. Paul's family was lucky in that his grandmother Anne, aged eighty-two, was still alive and in relatively good health.

"Bring me a photograph of her, please," Ruth requested during one of the drop offs. She had not dared to ask for anything of anyone in centuries, she realized.

Paul and Ruth spoke little about the mort resistance. The less she knew, the better. One day Alan will gain interest again in Ruth and her activities and he would be merciless in questioning her.

Throughout these months, a memory of the night of the fire, when they broke into LIFETECH plagued her, lingering in the background of her mind. She saw Marco's broken body beside her, his eyes open and unseeing. She knew he was dead, gone from her and Molly, and this was the worse realization she ever experienced. Two large security guards picked her up, and the pain was excruciating. Blood was falling into her eyes and her head ached as a constant ringing occurred. The guards tried to force her to stand on her own, but her leg buckled. She could tell that her left leg was badly injured as her hand limply brushed against her thigh. Her thigh felt wet and swollen; a sharp point protruding out from her torn pants. She tried to lift her left hand, but she couldn't move it above her waist. As the guards failed repeatedly to get Ruth stand on her own, they dragged her out of the room.

"Marco! Marco!" Ruth screamed. She screamed and cried, completely giving in to her horror. The love of her life was dead. Ruth wanted to join him; the pain was so bad, but she remembered Molly. She needed to return to her. She was thankful Marco insisted they leave Molly with his brother, Michael. Michael would hide Molly if he had to.

Ruth's broken body was dropped into a chair. She was now in an office, one she did not recognize. The guards tied her to the chair so that her body would not slide off. The pain now was so encompassing that she has no control over her body. To the guards' disgust, she wetted herself. Hot urine flowed down her pant leg, pooling amongst the bloody trail her body made when they dragged her to this chair. The grey carpet darkened beneath her.

Alan Blackmore stormed into the room. His face was angry; he could not keep his rage under control. He stood before her, gesturing ferociously.

"You will pay for this. I will track your family down and they will pay, too. Give me names of who else was involved." He kicked her broken leg, and she screamed.

"Talk, you bitch. Tell me something or we will roll your boyfriend out and dump him with the trash. It's not too late to help him." She knew Alan Blackmore was lying. Marco was dead; she saw his lifeless eyes. The bastard, Alan Blackmore, could did not even recall that Marco was her spouse after seven years of working for him. Hopefully, he won't learn about Molly.

"Talk." He screamed, and she felt his hot breath on her face. He slapped her hard across her temple over and over. Her blood splattered on him. He stopped eventually, exhausted. He recoiled when he noticed blood on his hands and clothing. She almost laughed as she saw he was standing now in a puddle of her urine and blood. Everything grew black, and he faded from her sight.

Alan Blackmore tried to question Ruth again weeks later. She was in a hospital; she was not sure exactly where. Her leg was enveloped in a cast. Bones in her leg, hip, and shoulder were pinned. Her face and head felt painfully swollen; she could hardly see out of her eyes. The ringing was still there, faint but constant. Ruth just wanted to die.

She saw no way out of this situation. She felt too broken to go find Molly. Molly is better off with Michael, she told herself.

"Give me names, Ruth Anderson." Alan commanded. He had time to calm down, but he was still so angry. Ruth could practically smell the fury on him. The crew must have successfully infected the servers before the fire overtook the floor. Ruth remembered bits and pieces of that night. The guards evacuated her, dragging her out again, careless of her injuries. Fire spread down the hall. She remembered the heat and the smoke before she felt the cool air outside the building. Then they dumped her in the back of a vehicle, slamming the door hard. She thought she would die in there, listening to the sirens.

Ruth was glad that she never changed her name with HR at LIFETECH after marrying Marco that week they discovered she was pregnant with Molly. Did she put

Molly's full name down with HR? She can't recall. Maybe Molly will have a chance, maybe he won't find her. Regardless, Guzman is a common name and the main building was destroyed by the fire; hopefully, this included the HR files on employees. Maybe they will never find Molly.

Alan had the doctor pump her full of drugs to get her to talk. It worked to a certain extent. Ruth babbled on about Marco, a baby, and her mother. She cried for her father, who died when she was a child. She cried and pleaded, but she had no names to offer up except a handful of first names — Carl, Rhonda, John. No one formally introduced themselves to her when Marco brought her aboard after she finally agreed to help Marco and the crew break into LIFETECH. She learnt a few of their first names, but suspected these names were not the true names of the people she helped into LIFETECH.

Then Alan Blackmore brought Ruth to his compound and set her up in the rooms, a roomy prison considering her crime against LIFETECH. She was certain he must have had her observed closely for years, decades even, recording everything she did and said. He must have found it all very dull as she was shattered, so deep in the fog of her depression, she did not care if she was alive or dead. Regardless, she had no information for him. Her role was to simply let the others into LIFETECH that fateful night and keep an eye out for the guards.

Chapter 9

Anthony Gelinas visited again at the end of August. He spoke with Ruth before she left the compound for her run.

"I am going to have you moved to my compound. Next week, though I wish I move you today."

Ruth did not reply. She looked into his face and saw his brow furrowed with concern. Who was this new Anthony, the Anthony who showed emotion?

"Ruth, the resistant is planning to ramp up their activities. It will anger the others. They will take it out on you. You will be safer with me."

"Alan will be suspicious. He would question why you want me back after all this time." Ruth said after a moment. She had that same question herself.

"I will tell him we fell in love again. Rekindled old flames and such. I have been working on some deals. I have something he wants. He can't refuse me."

Anthony and his secrecy. What deals? What would Alan want enough to sell her off to Anthony?

"Ruth, will you come with me? No strings attached. Our relation will be what you define it as. I truly want you to be safe." Anthony pleaded.

Ruth could see Anthony was afraid of something and he seemed genuine in his concern for her. She did not want to leave the area, though. She had ties here now with Paul and his family.

"Ruth, think about it. I plan to return next week to get you."

"Okay Anthony. I will think about it. I do have a condition. My family were buried here, my mother and father." Ruth lied. "Can I return to visit their graves?" Molly's burial site was near here; Ruth had learned that from Paul. Her parents were in the old city.

Anthony looked puzzled; she had never mentioned her parents in their time together. Ruth also never mentioned Molly or Marco.

"Yes, of course. I won't impose restrictions on you like the ones imposed here. I can't promise you absolute freedom, though. I don't even have that for myself, but I want to make things better. Please come with me."

Ruth saw again his naked fear on her behalf. It was genuine. She nodded, agreeing to return to him, and he visibly looked relieved. Though she agreed to move back with Anthony, she had doubts he would go through with this. It was best not to get her hopes up, that she could leave Blackmore compound.

Melissa's voice then reached their ears. Anthony moved in and kissed Ruth passionately, his hand grasping her hip towards him.

"Remember rekindled old flames. Play the game, Ruth," he whispered and planted another kiss.

Their bodies separated just as Melissa and Rob strolled by. The two others smirked and walked into the main house.

"Hello Ruth. I see Anthony is back in your life." Melissa made a beeline for her at supper. She herded Ruth into a corner of the dining room and motioned for her to sit down. Melissa was not subtle; it was not her style. Her expression was flat out probing as Melissa looked Ruth up and down.

"Yes, we started to talk again at the July party. He hasn't talked to Alan yet about us. Soon, I expect." Ruth said calmly. *Give Melissa what she wants, and she could be an ally.* Ruth could work with her.

"How romantic!" Melissa gushed sarcastically, checking Ruth over again as if she could dig out more details. Ruth felt the intensity of her gaze.

"Do you see any issues, you know, that Alan may have? I know he is not the biggest fan of Anthony." Ruth tested the waters. *Draw Melissa in, pretend to share and she will be amenable.*

"I wouldn't know. Alan does as Alan wants, as we all do — what Alan wants," Melissa responded flippantly, her face hard underneath the glittery makeup. Then, she softened a bit and added, "But Ruth, I do hope things work out for you. You have been kind when others have not been." Melissa stiffened as if she was caught in a bad memory.

"In another time, I might have called you a friend." Melissa surprised Ruth with this unexpected comment.

"Thank you, Melissa, I wish you well too." Strange thing was Ruth wished Melissa well. Was it the loneliness? Or perhaps she saw Melissa as a younger colleague or even a sister she wanted to help. What choices did Melissa really have in her life? Alan's offer of immortality to Melissa — or more importantly the offer to leave the poverty and confinement of a mort life — must have been so appealing to a half starved, clever young woman like Melissa. Melissa was just as trapped as Ruth, and they both understood this.

Ruth increased her transcribing time. She wrote for an extra hour each day. Her hand cramped and her eyes ached from the effort. Ruth almost completed the list, though. Wednesday, she went out as usual; it was a cooler day with short periods of rain. Paul was there. This time, he was not alone. An elderly woman was behind him, sitting on a fallen log.

"Ruth, this is my grandmother, Anne Guzman." The old woman rose gingerly and motioned Ruth towards her. Arms stretched out and Ruth moved in, feeling the fragile yet solid embrace of the older woman. They held each other under the shade of the trees. Birds sang in the canopy of the woods above them. Anne remined Ruth of her own mother. The resemblance was uncanny.

"My grandfather talked about his grandmother, Molly. We also heard stories of you, imprisoned in that house. We weren't certain, though, if it was really you, the Ruth who was at the LIFETECH fire."

Ruth lingered as long as she could, just holding the old woman's hand; the rain stopped, and the woods glistened green and gold. Being in the presence of an older person was a rarity, like seeing a solar eclipse or northern lights. Being in the presence of your deceased daughter's great

great grandchild was unreal, bittersweet. *My Molly, my Molly.*

A parent should never have to bury their child. This sad thought haunted Ruth for centuries. Ruth often felt as though she was frozen, trapped, in this body of a thirty-something. She did not have the luxury of growing further and aging, of moving on from a moment of time. She was stuck, forced to watch the world creep past her. But at this moment, being in the presence of her descendants, of someone who connected to her Molly, it was a tether. These people brought the spirit of Marco and Molly back to the present, into the light of day.

Time passed too quickly. Ruth had hung on to every word Anne said, memorized every detail of the old woman's face. Again, she was struck how Anne resembled an older version of her mother. She let Paul and Anne do most of the talking, telling Ruth family stories. Ruth heard how their ancestors moved out of the old city into Richmond, using false names for decades until they realized no one was looking for them. Michael Guzman had established a food bank and Molly became a nurse. Many of the family members went into medical services. Access to formal education was restricted, so most morts were apprenticed. Anne herself was a midwife.

Soon Paul, Anne, and Ruth had to part. They had spent twenty minutes together; any longer would alert Blackmore security. Ruth left first, waving as she started her run back to the Blackmore compound. *Today, I got back some of what I lost, family. I belong to them, Paul and Anne.* Her heart felt light, dizzily so, and she wanted to sing out to the birds, the chattering squirrels, and chipmunks.

Chapter 10

The time had come and Anthony had returned as he promised. Ruth had flopped back and forth on how she felt; a large part of her regretted telling him she would leave with him. She wanted to tell him today she wanted to stay at the Blackmore compound. Ruth was afraid of getting too close to Anthony. She also did not want to leave the compound where Paul was working. In the end, though, Ruth chose to say nothing, letting Anthony move forward with his plan. She would leave Blackmore compound with Anthony this morning.

Ruth packed a small bag with her art supplies, some of her favourite texts, and the prized photograph. She reasoned that if Alan and the others discovered she had contact with the morts and, worse, that she was connected to them, they would punish the morts at the compound and in the settlement. Ruth could not bear the idea of harm coming to Paul and Anne. She also trusted Anthony's concerns; if a mort resistant was active near the Blackmore compound, it would be very risky for her to be in Alan's presence. Ruth would be one of the first to experience Alan's retaliation.

To help time pass as she waited for Anthony in her room, she picked up the datapad and read a familiar novel by Jane Austen, *Persuasion*, one she read in high school. She sat on the chair by the window. The sky was a beautiful rich blue with white clouds streaking across. Soon the trees would turn gold and red and then the leaves would fall. Winter over the last three centuries was much milder from the winters of her childhood, but the seasons still changed — summer to fall to winter to spring. Time moved forward even when she could not.

A knock at the door and Melissa entered. Melissa, of course, did not want to miss Alan Blackmore's reaction when Ruth left again, Ruth mused. Only fifty years passed for Melissa and she already sunk into the numbing boredom of the halted. Today promised some drama. Melissa watched Ruth smooth her top and head towards the door, leaving her suite to hopefully for the last time.

"Courage Ruth, courage." Melissa gave a sad smile. Melissa appeared old for a split second, years beyond her halted age of twenty; the weary look of her eyes contrasted with her smooth face and impeccably styled hair. Melissa's words of encouragement were unexpected kindness, so unlike her.

Melissa escorted Ruth to Alan's main office. Ruth felt a pang of anxiety when she had to hand over her suitcase to a mort receptionist outside the office. The office itself was a room of metal and glass, a stark pallet of black and white. Anthony sat on a leather couch, his arm casually resting on the back. She admired how calm and collect he portrayed himself. He patted the spot for her to sit beside him. She sat, stiff and awkward, her leg against Anthony's leg. Alan Blackmore, who was standing, moved to sit opposite of them.

"You can go Melissa." Alan ordered Melissa to leave the room. He too appeared calm but failed to emit the casual coolness Anthony possessed.

"Apparently, your love has renewed, so Anthony tells me. He is willing to pay a high price to move you from us here. I take it you feel the same. You have feelings for Anthony?"

High price? Ruth puzzled over that.

"Yes sir. I ask you to allow me to leave with him." Ruth nearly choked on her words, but grovelling was a strategy that had a high rate of success with Alan.

"Anthony, I cannot let her go. Ruth remains here. She is mine, my employee. We go way back, don't we, little mouse?"

Anthony shifted beside Ruth. Without directly looking at him, Ruth knew he was angry.

"Alan, I am giving you most of my shares. You will have the lion's half of LIFETECH finally after all this time. You need this, you know it, otherwise Bethany will plow you down."

Alan appeared unmoved. His eyes then narrowed as he glared at the two of them.

"Let her go. I say, let her go." Then, in a softer tone, Anthony said, "I will give up fully my position on the board. All my shares. You will stand unchallenged, but she goes today with me."

Alan's face registered a moment of surprise at Anthony's persistence.

"Anthony, you are a fool. She is hardly worth it."

"Then let her go with me. Why hang on to her all this time?" Anthony folded his arms across his long legs. "I shouldn't have brought her back. You pressured the board to force her to return here. Why? What was your game, Alan? Why can't you let that fire go? It hardly stopped LIFETECH."

Ruth was stunned and looked at Anthony. Anthony did not willingly end their relationship all those years ago.

"Alan, do you accept the terms? I want an answer now."

Alan smiled like he was the winner.

"Yes, get out of here, both of you. Anthony, I expect your resignation to the board immediately."

Anthony grabbed Ruth's arm forcibly and pulled her out of the room. "We need to go now."

"My suitcase," Ruth thought of the photograph hidden in there. She had tucked it deep into a book, but she still feared someone would find it.

"We just pushed Alan to his limit. We need to go now." He signalled for his bodyguards; he brought two into the house and they are clearly armed, weapon holsters bulging under their jackets. Melissa was hovering in the hallway.

"Ruth, here you go." She handed over the precious suitcase to Ruth.

"Thanks." Ruth touched Melissa's hand as a slight gesture of gratitude.

In the backseat of the dark sedan, hidden from the outside by tinted windows, Ruth took a long look at the main house, the grounds, and the gatehouse. She wanted to be happy, but the last time she thought she was leaving for good, she ended up returning. And then she saw Paul out on the grounds. It pained her to think that she might not see him again.

Paul, dressed in the gardener's outfit, was riding the lawn mower. She touched the glass window. He would not know it was her in the vehicle. Hopefully, a mort staff member will tell him she left the compound; still, Ruth wanted to roll down the window but she let her hand drop to her side. Anthony, lost in his own thoughts, did not notice Ruth. The vehicle left the compound gate and his hand gripped hers tight.

In the leather luxury of the sedan, the two of them were alone. A thick glass partition separated them from his security detail. An awkward silence enveloped them.

Anthony looked at the partition, then he looked at her.

"I am going to bring LIFETECH down. Then the others. I needed you to be away from them before I start the work."

"What are you saying? You are them. You are a part of LIFETECH."

"Ruth, there are a lot of us, the halted, who are frankly just tired. I am not saying I grew a conscious finally, got a moral compass. But maybe I am, maybe I am suffering from a conscious. I'm coming up on three hundred years of so-called living. It weighs on me, what LIFETECH did. What I did. We are stunted. We are dead inside and a cancer on this planet. Something needs to change. Some of us are planning. Hopefully, we can knock enough of them down so the morts can at least stand a chance. Life is for living. The halted are not living."

It was the most passion and feeling Ruth saw in a halted, other than Alan's anger. That anger, Alan's rage, dulled, though, over the centuries. She doubted any halted, fully felt emotions, including herself, except maybe loneliness. Ruth so wanted to trust Anthony, but something inside herself prevented her. She patted his hand and let him half embrace her. He kissed desperately kissed her, still overcome by his own emotions. Ruth would not tell him of her scribing or of Paul and her mort descendants — not until she was certain she could trust him.

When Anthony released her and leaned back against his side of the vehicle seat, Ruth checked if he had composed himself. Anthony's eyes were closed and he looked tired but calm.

"I have a lot of questions, Anthony. I don't know where to begin. What are you going to do without a position in LIFETECH?"

"I sold my European properties. I have a couple of small businesses that make a decent profit. Most of which even LIFETECH is not aware of. Ruth, I have always been lucky with money. Still, I safeguarded as much as I could before going to talk to Alan. I knew he would want me out of LIFETECH before he let you go. Let's just say I have been working on this exit plan for decades. I needed to be sure we can get away and then stay away."

"What about what you said to Alan? What did you mean when you said you were forced to end things with us?"

Anthony's face drooped with exhaustion; he looked much older in that moment.

"I don't know how to begin, Ruth. I wanted to be with you. Back then, I convinced Alan to let you leave. Of course, it cost me, but your companionship meant everything to me. The others seemed ok with us. Alan seemed ok too. He had his own interests at that time, pursuing Bethany, as I recall. I thought he had forgotten his obsession to punish you for that day, the fire. But time passed, and he grew very resentful that I was happy and content. That you were, I hope, happy. You were happy?" He looked hesitantly at Ruth. Ruth froze, unsure of what to say.

"Well, the board confronted me without Alan." Anthony continued, now uncomfortable by her silence. "He was causing too much trouble for the others and they wanted to make a peace offering. I was maybe a little insecure about us. Maybe I feared you had grown tired of our life together. Pressure built; they were prepared to destroy me financially. This was before I diversified my assets, learnt to hide my money. We would have had no protection. I don't know if you know how dangerous that is — a halted with no money. The board all swore they would ensure your safety. Rob swore to me personally he would watch out for you. I caved and I guess Alan was satisfied to know that I was miserable without you. It was enough for Alan, for a while. He started to play ball again with the rest of the board. I bided my time, planning to come back for you. It's time now. Damn LIFETECH and the Council."

Chapter 11

Ruth found herself set up in another series of rooms in another compound. This compound was two hours' drive north, beside the ocean, up a forested cliff. Ruth's first impression was the Gelinas compound was a beautiful villa style estate, smaller than Blackmore's compound, but just as heavily guarded. Anthony purchased this compound after their relationship had ended the first time.

Her rooms were beautiful with a view that including the ocean and the settlement of Richmond to the south. That comforted her, knowing Anne and Paul were out there, beyond her windows. The sitting area had French doors to the deck. Anthony's suite also opened onto the same deck. Below, she saw his collection of yachts. She doubted he still had the same one all this time that they had travelled together on before. She imagined that particular boat was out of commission, rusting.

Ruth arranged her items and hung up her clothes. The photograph of Molly and Michael sat out in the open on her nightstand. She planned to ask Anthony for a frame to hold it properly. Ruth would have to sit down with Anthony one day and tell him about Marco and Molly, maybe even find a way to explain about Paul and Anne. Maybe she could find a mort artist to render it on canvas. She did not trust the shadow of her former artist skill; the result would be wooden.

Ruth felt a small ray of hope and she tried to suppress it. Based on experience, she had no logical reason to feel a glimmer of hope. However, the sun was shining. The walls of her new room glittered. She moved outside onto the balcony, listening to the distant waves below. Seagulls, small white shapes above, flew in circles. Their cries echoed in the gentle breeze. Hope was not a plan of action, Marco had said often when he begged her to take a side, to fight back, and help them with their plan of sabotage. Hope was all she really had — hope and the memories of Marco and Molly, and all the people she loved and left behind in her old life.

Ruth learnt of Marco's involvement with a resistant group a year after she completed parental leave and returned to LIFETECH. This group went beyond organizing protests and handing out leaflets. When she questioned him, Marco admitted he had joined shortly before Molly's birth.

"I can't just sit by and let the corporations, especially your LIFETECH, erode what ever safety nets we had. We are losing our rights, Ruth; our opportunities are shrinking. You have to admit that people, such as you and me, are seeing our salaries decrease and what ever benefits too. If we have another child, neither of us has any medical insurance, thanks to the latest rollback. The rich get wealthier and we get poorer. I don't want that for Molly!" Marco lectured her. She had heard it multiple times. He was always vocal about his anger at the state of affairs. Coupled with his encyclopedic memory of labour history, he was unbearable during these rants. He was on track to be a professor in labour studies, but the department was cut dramatically after he completed his master's program.

"I know, I do. But I live in the now, Marco. I need that job to feed Molly and us." Ruth also secretly liked it at LIFETECH: the pristine, clean offices, the friendly banter amongst her colleagues, and the potential for advancement. Advancement was slim, but there was some hope. LIFETECH was one of the top ten corporations worldwide. It was rapidly gaining influence with the mass exodus in Silicon Valley. The intense heat, coupled by drought and wildfires, saw the American industries move north.

LIFETECH was one of those Silicon Valley corporations that made an early move up to Vancouver. The media referred to LIFETECH and many other tech corporations that moved into Canada as Silicon Valley North.

But overall, it was the sense of security Ruth received when she walked through the glass doors and through the metal detectors that she liked best. The world was chaotic with riots and protests. There was so much division. LIFETECH was an oasis from the hard reality and she willingly ignored its role in creating the present state. Until now, when she discovered Marco's recent activities, she had no problem compartmentalizing her life at LIFETECH and her life with Marco.

"Ruth, you can't say you know nothing about the halting. They have been experimenting on poor people, homeless people mostly, just so they can live a couple of decades. Fucking vain, evil maniacal two bit villains. And then there are the groups who want to upload their consciousness to a super frame. As if they had a conscious! These people are controlling our planet and we are hostage to them. Something's got to be done."

"Marco, be careful. I need you; Molly needs you." Ruth then started to cry. Marco prepared himself to leave the apartment. It was 11:30 pm, and he was in dark pants and a black hoodie. He wouldn't tell her where he was heading, and she really did not want to know. He returned home, wired, after six am. Just enough time for him to eat and shower, and then head out to his day job. Molly was awake and she clamoured to the kitchen table as he made coffee for the day.

"Daddy! Where were you?" Molly asked, in the happy loud child voice a six-year old child had, but then she was distracted by the glass of juice Ruth handed her. Best to leave that question unanswered.

Marco turned on the radio and searched for a news program. They long ago cancelled any cable package because of the expense. A serious male voice — typical newscaster style — spoke of breaking news. Terrorists destroyed the UPLOAD industrial plant. A security guard was seriously injured; no deaths reported. Marco listened intently as Ruth left the room so Molly would not notice how upset she was. UPLOAD was that company Marco said was rumoured to have discovered a way to upload the human consciousness. Marco accused them of bilking stupid, old rich people of their money who allowed UPLOAD to freeze their heads like morbid popsicles for some distance future utopia.

Ruth had to devise a new daily routine, one that included Anthony now. He, out of respect, kept a polite distance, but he was eager to join her in activities — walks, swims in the pool. He asked if he could join her on her runs and, together, they discovered new trails. Anthony was not as disciplined or practiced as Ruth, so she slowed her pace down considerably and cut the distances significantly. They shared every meal together and spent most mornings reading in comfortable silence. Anthony's passion was book collecting. His prized item was a medieval manuscript of the Canterbury Tales. He made her wash her hand before he allowed her to turn the pages. She was in awe of the short bold lines forming letters, carefully crafted between faded charcoal lines. Anthony enthusiastically showed her the scribbles and sketches in the margins — the doodling of some ancient monk amidst the strenuous hours it took to complete a page of text.

She had not returned yet to her own texts and transcribing. She was putting off the decision whether to continue or not. There was a small mort settlement ten kilometres away. Perhaps she could have a vehicle drive her to the Richmond settlement. Perhaps she could somehow establish contact with Paul again. She still owed him one last text from the list, an old biography about a founder of Silicon Valley.

By the second week, Ruth brought Anthony to her sitting room. They had finished a small breakfast on the deck; below the leaves in the trees were yellowing. She took out a stack of her writings from her literature phase. She handed him her transcription of old poems, Shakespeare's sonnets. He marvelled at her tight cursive, which filled the pages. Unlike his collection, there were no notations in the margins. Ruth would not have trusted herself. She might have written a message to some unknown reader about Marco and Molly. She might have bared her soul only to have it used against her by Alan Blackmore and the others.

"I can't read it, Ruth. Who reads cursive these days? But it is beautiful." He traced some of the words with his finger.

"I will teach you."

Anthony cupped her face and kissed her. She kissed him back.

That night, she dreamt of Marco on their wedding day. They were giddy and happy as they headed to City Hall for a civil marriage. Ruth found a beautiful creamed coloured dress her size at the thrift shop. It was an amazing find! So lovely! She figured she was nearly three months pregnant and so far, the only changes were her breasts; they were fuller and tender to the touch. She thought her belly looked larger, but Marco said he didn't notice much of a difference.

Marco's mother, Anna, came; she was almost as happy as the couple. They toyed with the idea of a slightly larger ceremony with a couple of close friends and Michael, but, as long as Marco had her mother there, he was content. And that was good enough for Ruth.

Marco looked handsome in an old suit he borrowed from Micheal. Black with grey pinstripes, a lovely silk tie that belonged to his father. His father died when Marco was a small child — a factory accident. Anna received almost compensation to put both boys through university. Ruth and Marco had that in common, the loss of their fathers. Ruth's father died in a vehicle accident when she was a small child, too. Then she lost her mother because of cancer while Ruth was attending university. So much lost, it moulded Ruth's life, but now they had something to celebrate — their marriage and an upcoming baby. There was hope in the air.

Ruth danced with Marco in the kitchen, playing old favourites from high school and uni. She was drunk on love as she was too afraid to drink alcohol with the fetus in her body. She so wanted to do good by this baby. Marco kissed Ruth over and over and then he picked her up, cradling her body in both arms, and headed to the bedroom. Ruth has had this dream a million times, except now Marco morphed into Anthony and then back into himself. Anthony was spinning around the kitchen with her, then Marco, back to Anthony. It was Anthony carrying her to their bed, and she was happy. Could she love another person?

Chapter 12

It was the end of September, and the cliffs have streaks of golden and red amongst the evergreens. Fall was in full swing. Ruth wondered where Anthony was. He left the compound after breakfast with two security guards, saying very little about where he was headed. Anthony's staff, others and morts like, were silent about Anthony's absence. His staff was respectful to Ruth but they did not offer up any information.

Now that she found herself alone, she wondered what risks he put himself at by giving up his position at LIFETECH. Alan Blackmore and the others were vindictive and petty. If they thought Anthony was a threat, they would take action. Ruth heard rumours through the decades about the assassination of others. Anthony must clearly have that concern as his compound had more security guards, even security dogs, than the Blackmore compound, certainly more than when she previously lived with him. He paid his mort staff well and worked at good relations, there by encouraging loyalty to him. This was a far cry from the oppressive atmosphere at Alan Blackmore's compound. Ruth noticed, though, a sense of anticipation hung in the air.

Lunch hour came and no Anthony. Ruth took a security guard with her and walked down the steep cliff to the beach. Anthony insisted Ruth have security when she left the compound. Molly would have loved this — the beach, the ocean waves. Ruth imagined a young Molly stomping in the water and skipping stones into the ocean. Ruth picked a couple of shells to show Anthony later; she selected the most intact ones she could find — white on the outside, iridescent pink on the inside. She second guessed her action. Why would Anthony care about seashells? She decided to ignore her insecurity and pocketed the seashells for later.

Supper hour came and passed, and Ruth was flat out worried. Anthony owed nothing to her — his schedule was his own — but he was usually considerate of her during the past weeks. He seemed reluctant to spend any time away from her and the compound. Funny, after so many decades of being utterly alone, she had grown used to people around such as Paul and Anthony. She even wondered about Melissa; she hoped Melissa was well.

Ruth went to Anthony's offices and spoke to his mort assistant, John Reilly, inquiring when Anthony would return.

"He did not say, ma'am. Shall I text him for you? Tomorrow I will inquire about getting you your own smartphone. I am sure Mr. Gelinas had planned to purchase one for you by now."

The morts here were polite to Ruth, a far cry from the Blackmore compound. She was free to walk around the compound. It took a bit to get used to.

"Thank you, John," Ruth replied. "I can wait. I was just missing his presence."

Feeling a bit guilty from the weeks of relative leisure she had after decades of a strict routine, Ruth planned to swim laps in the outdoor pool after supper and then head to bed. It felt good to exhaust her body with physical exertion. As she dressed for bed, Ruth mentally reminded herself to stay sharp. She did not want to lose the gains in fitness she worked hard to get; it was the only edge she had over the others. This can't last forever, she rued, this peaceful life with Anthony. She turned the light off on her nightstand and laid her head on the pillow.

Anthony! She woke up in the middle of the night screaming his name. Images of the others torturing him played over and over. Alan Blackmore's angry face hovered over Anthony. The last image before she woke was of Anthony, broken and bloodied on the ground, legs and feet kicking and stomping at him.

A knock at her door. She threw on a robe and opened the door to find Anthony, alive and well. His expression was one of concern; he must have heard her screams through the wall.

"Bad dream," she said sheepishly, inviting him in. She was sweaty and hot.

"I remember you used to have quite a few bad dreams." He touched her arm, and she embraced him, so thankful he was safe before her. She kissed him hard and led him to the bed, pulling his body towards her. Afterwards, Ruth slept dreamlessly beside Anthony.

In the morning, Anthony asked Ruth to come to his offices. She sat while he served coffee. She did not know what to expect. A knock at the door sounded, and a halted assistant, Rick, opened the door. In walked Paul. Ruth gasped, clutching the armrests of the chair.

"Ruth, I'm glad to see you again." Paul reached out to hold her hand and then sat beside her when she refused to touch him.

"Anthony, what is going on?" Ruth said, looking between both men. Her heart pumped loudly. She stood straight up, ready to bolt.

"Ruth, I met with Paul Foster last night. He mentioned he connected with you at Blackmore's compound. Do you remember our conversations about my group? The halted who want to end the Corporations control? I know I haven't told you much, but we finally brokered an agreement with a mort resistance group. We met yesterday in person. Paul is one of the leaders." Anthony explained.

"My group has members working in the Blackmore Compound. We have been working there for years now. I have members in housekeeping, serving staff, even security. You saw how I moved about. The others there don't really notice much. They don't see us morts as people. My group, we are preparing for a series of attacks. We knew Mr. Gelinas' group was sympathetic to our cause, so we are taking our chances and combining efforts." Paul added.

Ruth looked both men over. She felt dizzy, uncertain of what to say.

"I have been upfront with you, Ruth, that I am tired of the status quo. I am disgusted with LIFETECH and the Council, the halted — myself especially. There are quite a few of us feel this way. We need to break the Council and the Corporations, starting with LIFETECH. I needed you out of the way, to be safe, so we can actively fight the Council." Anthony said as he tried to hold Ruth's hand, but she stiffened up. Ruth's head swam in confusion and fear. Paul moved to sit closer to her, his face frowning with concerned. Anthony noticed their familiarity with each other.

"Paul Foster, how exactly do you know Ruth?" Anthony questioned, tense now as if he was ready to attack the mort man, "You two seem to know each other more than you indicated."

"He is my great, great, and so on, grandson, Anthony. Four greats, we counted. My daughter Molly's descendant." Ruth spoke quietly before Paul could answer.

"Ruth and me here, we are related; we're family," Paul added.

Chapter 13

Life was odd, Ruth thought to herself as she woke the next day. The wake-up program went off like it did every other day, the gradual increase in light, the birdsong. Outside, the seagulls cried out as if in competition with the recording. Anthony laid beside her, still sleeping soundly. Ruth realized that someday soon she would have to sort out her feelings for this man and reconcile them with her memories of Marco. Anthony was not like Marco. Marco was a fiery, passionate man who lived by a strict, unwavering moral code that judged all, including his own wife, against his impossible standard. Anthony was late to the party when it came to using a moral compass, but he was kind to Ruth and accepted her as she was. He accepted what little Ruth could offer with a quiet appreciation. Prehalt, Anthony was one of those high-speed, type A male from an upper middle class — a corporate success story. Ruth was on the bottom of the rungs in her old life, just wanting to focus on her survival and that of her child and spouse until she lost it all. Back then, their lives did not intersect, not even at LIFETECH. Now, in the uncertain direction they were heading as Anthony looked to unseat LIFETECH, they were equals in a sense. Ruth and Anthony were two humans living in this surreal world, tired of the loneliness and the lack of human compassion.

Anthony struggled to believe the family connection between Paul and Ruth; it sounded too incredible. Paul argued it was basic math. Ruth had Molly, Molly had two children, those children had children and so on. Ruth had over a hundred of direct descendants as a result living today. Because of Molly, Marco and Ruth lived on, at least parts of their genes did. Ruth went and grabbed the photo at her bedstand. Anthony saw for himself that the woman in the photography. Parts of Molly looked like Ruth and Paul;

Ruth's face shape, Paul's eyes. All three had a similar stance. After that, Anthony accepted the reality of Ruth's genuine connection with Paul.

Strangely, it felt like Ruth was bringing stepchildren to their, Ruth and Anthony's, relationship, if she could be so bold to define her feelings for him. Anthony now had to decide if he could handle a family. At this moment, it seemed like he tentatively accepted the reality of Ruth's family. Anthony was turning the idea around in his head and looking at Ruth through a different lens.

After lunch, Anthony and Paul closed the office door and sent Ruth away. They had a lot of work to do. It was a strange déjà vu feeling, like how Marco would depart for his meetings with the protest group and then the resistant group. This time, though, Ruth had no job, no bills, and no rent to worry about. She had no child or spouse who depended on her to keep safe. Ruth had nothing to justify her inaction. *I was foolish to think my scribing did anything to help*; she chastised herself. Ruth wondered if she was brave enough to act now, if she had the strength. *I want to do something for Marco and Molly, for Paul and Anne.*

Later that evening, Ruth was alone with Anthony; he seemed exhilarated. He had a purpose and a cause. His joy was infectious. She could love this Anthony, the Anthony centuries away for the suited executive at LIFETECH. She loved him; Ruth realized. They made love that night with a renewed sense of vigour.

In the middle of the night, Ruth woke — another dream. This time, she dreamt of her dad tucking her into bed. She would have been four or five. It was hard for her to recall his face. She only remembered the solidness of him, the comfort she felt when he held her or sat beside her. As the dream faded, she rested on her side and watched Anthony lay sleeping. His face was peaceful. He stirred and opened his eyes, blinking in the dark. He smiled when he saw Ruth was awake beside him.

"I want to help. Surely, I can do something. You know I can run. I can write. Useful for secret codes, I guess. Seriously, can you find a place for me?" Ruth asked Anthony, sitting up in the bed.

He shifted to see her more clearly.

"If that is what you want. Of course."

Chapter 14

Paul began to visit every day. He took up lodgings in a small settlement nearby. Every day he reported to the gate early each morning, dressed like a labourer, part of Anthony's mort staff. Anthony was determined to hide any sign of resistance as long as he could; he feared LIFETECH was observing him. The halted community could not understand how he would just walk away with all that power and wealth — surely not for a woman with no significance, only noteworthy as the one who was involved in the fire at LIFETECH.

Anthony continued to make changes to the staff at this compound. He sent two halted members, Rick Huhn and Mike Spenser, to oversee his other properties in the Interior and on the coast. He also reduced many of the mort staffs such as housekeeping in order to ensure privacy.

Meanwhile, Anthony bolstered his security. He started these changes slowly over the last ten years; he explained to Ruth. When he was confident that his remaining staff, halted and mort alike, were trustworthy, he started planning the resistant in earnest in the recent years and reaching out to other like-minded halted and then to Paul's group.

Ruth noticed an increase visitors, morts and halted persons, entering the compound daily. Anthony's staff set up a planning room on the lower floor, using the formal dining room. Bedrooms were converted into office spaces.

There were two key aspects to the planning. The first aspect involved an once brilliant scientist, a halted man from LIFETECH's chief rival, Genesis. A couple of exceptionally bright morts aided the scientist in developing a biological virus. This plan involved spreading the virus to as many halted individuals as possible throughout the continent and then spread it worldwide. The purpose of the virus was to alter the genetic coding of the halted and kick-start the aging process, ending the halt. The plan also focused on deploying many teams to spread the virus, as well as targeting the major servers that provided the digi-medic updates. It was crucial that the digi-medics could not detect the purpose of the virus until the virus affected most halted.

The second aspect to planning was more scorch earth. A mort leader had devised an Electronic Magnetic pulse bomb. She was working on manufacturing several in order to shut down electrical grids and disrupt communication systems. This plan too required teams to deploy around the continent to detonate the bombs. Many feared EMP bombs would hurt mort settlements, especially essential services such as medical centres. The groups had to devise mitigation plans such as supplying mort communities with back up generators.

From what Ruth was able to gleam, the mort resistance was larger and more widespread than she could ever imagine. They quietly prepared for war.

Arguments broke out in the Gelinas compound. Who should lead? How should they organize? The morts distrusted Anthony and the other halted, but they needed their knowledge of the halted community and their money. Anthony and his group wanted change, but they feared what their new roles in the future would be. They feared losing their positions of privilege. They also, despite all their attempts to change, did not view the morts fully as their equals. As such, there were several impasses the two groups had to overcome to proceed with a coordinated effort.

In October, one of the halted who worked in the Council, the governing halted body, warned that the corporations were lowering the age for mort workers in the mines and industrial farms. There were plans to limit mort schools to age fourteen from sixteen in the North and South Americas. All were aware of reports of increasingly violent riots regarding the rationing of food staples in Europe. The Council which controlled the North and South Americas wanted to create tighter restrictions on morts to avoid European riots. Protests and riots frequently occurred on the continent here, but authorities had quickly quashed them so far. The current strict laws regarding mort assemblies helped the halted control of the Americas, but the Council still felt threatened.

Ruth, despite her request to help, found herself without much of an official role. Unofficially, she assisted Anthony in every way she could. Ruth prepared agendas, took notes, and helped him draft proposals. She calmed frayed nerves. She acted as an intermediatory between Paul and his group and the halted. For those who listened, she described what happened before the halting, what she knew of Marco's role in the pre-halt resistance. Ruth wished she knew more about Marco's exploits. If Marco was here right now, Ruth thought frequently, he would have plans and ideas. Marco would easily fall into a leadership role.

One morning, she noticed a new person. It was a mort from Alan Blackmore's compound, one of the housekeeping staff. She was the middle-aged woman who often brought in her meals back at Blackmore compound, the one who glared at her fiercely as she rolled in a cart with breakfast or lunch. Ruth learnt Paul had recruited this woman to collect information at the Blackmore compound. The woman, Linda, acknowledged Ruth with a slight nod. She would be returning to the Blackmore compound to continue spying that evening.

"Can we trust her?" Ruth asked Paul, remembering the scowls and hostile attitude Ruth endured from this woman. Paul nodded.

"I have known Linda my whole life. Her partner died twenty years ago when a group of halted went to the Richmond settlement looking to stir up trouble for entertainment. They ganged up on Linda and her partner, Rose. Rose was beaten so badly, she went into a coma and died. Our hospital had a power outage at the time and couldn't provide proper care. Probably led to Rose's death. Linda wants change, like the rest of us."

Chapter 15

One week in later October, boxes arrived at Anthony's compound. It was weapons and various military style equipment. Paul insisted everyone, including Anthony and his halted conspirators, needed to train to fight. He had planned a boot camp of sorts for all the halted at the compound, taught by Paul himself and a group of six other morts. Ruth and Anthony found themselves learning how to handle small arms and to conduct basic fighting — close quarter combat, as Paul called it. Ruth wanted to giggle every time she picked up the magnetic pulse rifle or the ancient magazine fed handguns and rifles. The heavy weight of the weapons felt so foreign in her hands. She never imagined being a soldier. That was someone other than her. Someone strong and fierce. Someone like Marco.

Ruth found though she enjoyed learning the drills of assembling and firing, fault finding and dissembling. She appreciated the order of the drills. Most of the lessons occurred on the lower floors of the great house in which hasty classrooms were created. The oil and carbon that caked on the steel of the rifle stained Ruth's hands, and she had to work on acquiring the hand strength required to operate the weapons. Her shoulders and arms ached as she held the rifle firm against her right shoulder. Ruth practiced the drills over and over, as commanded by Paul and the other morts. Even in her dreams, she went over drills — loading and unloading, stripping, and cleaning. Anthony worked beside her, quiet in concentration as he worked on cleaning an old pistol with an old rag. Their eyes locked, and they laughed at their predicament; they compared their dirty hands and bragged about sore muscles.

The winter rains had begun, but Paul coerced the motley group outside to teach them some basic survival. Paul and the other instructors showed an impressive amount of patience with the halted. They had to teach them very basic concepts repeatedly, like how to dress to stay warm and dry, and yet not overheat. The morts taught the halted group how to move tactically through the house, the grounds, and the woods. Anthony's group and Ruth learnt about improvised shelters and how to conceal themselves. They wrestled with each other and attacked makeshift mannikins with knifes and bayonets.

To Ruth's surprise, and the halted and morts, she was a quick learner. Paul complimented her as such when she adeptly stripped and reassembled the ancient rifle.

"Teacher's pet!" a halted woman, Tessa, called out, and the group laughed, even Ruth herself.

The group crowded together in Anthony's dining room for lunch. His cook made marvellous soups and stews that chased the chill of the day away. Everyone ate with relish. During these meals, Ruth finally got to know Anthony's core group of halted: Luke Grant, Stephen Unger, Alexandra Chen, James Holland, Tessa Montague, Dale Platonov, Bruce Roberts. Mike Spencer and Rick Huhn also rejoined them at the compound for this training. Ruth also got to know many of the mort staff, including John Reilly and the cook, Abigail Wise.

On a day that rain poured steadily throughout, the group conducted a range shoot out in the far corner of the property. It was truly cold and miserable. Ruth's hands were blue and achy; she struggled to grip the weapon and to complete the drills competently. She could not stop shivering. The wet seeped into her inner clothes and moved down her back.

"I know, I know," Paul barked at the group; everyone was soaking wet. "We need the cover of the rain to prevent prying eyes. Regardless, this might save your lives. We can't depend on nice weather in a war."

The boot camp was over after five weeks. Ruth thought she saw a subtle shift in Anthony and the other halted. Their sense of purpose grew. They talked more openly with the morts. On the mort side, a sliver of trust was earned towards Anthony's halted. They all, the morts and the halted, had a long way to go, but Ruth felt a sense of community and fellowship tentatively emerge.

July was chosen as the official launch date for the resistance. The confirmation of the official launch of the resistance was made through the mort networks. Ruth had learned about the highly effective lines of communications the morts developed. The morts relied on word of mouth, radio, and persons operating as dispatch carriers.

Communication among the morts was surprisingly quick. Ruth was pleased to learn that a lot of morts used cursive to code messages based on the texts she left. She also learnt that a lot of her transcriptions spread throughout the Americas and into Europe.

Anthony and the halted group had their fleets of private airplanes and yachts. They still used the halted communications — smart phones and the internet. They tried to be careful, to hide their true intentions. Paul frequently cautioned the halted about the possibility of these luxuries being taken away or somehow betraying them. Anthony's halted all would have to learn to live without the halted advantages in the future. Ruth tried to imagine Anthony without his fancy home or the luxury vehicles in his garages. She tried to imagine him without his speed boats or yachts. She was unsuccessful, and if she had to be honest with herself, she wondered if she could hack it in a world without the halted advantages she lived with for so long.

Anthony and Paul talked often about the July launch of the resistance. They planned to attack key areas simultaneously after releasing the virus. The major Northern American Corporations — all who owned positions on the Council — would be targeted first. The resistance would temporarily dismantle their servers and power grids and apprehend key leadership. Meanwhile, the virus would continue to spread among the halted. A coalition government would step in and unite the morts and its halted allies. Anthony was working with Paul to create a framework for this coalition.

Ruth tried to imagine all of this — this grand plan. It was hard for her, though, to fully comprehend it all and see her role in it, so she did what she knew best. She ran every day, pushing her body to move fast. Anthony no longer joined her; he was preoccupied with his planning sessions with

Paul, the other morts, and his trusted halted. Ruth was free to run as long as she wanted. She ran often in the rain and wind along the cliffs overlooking the ocean and the mort settlement. The seagulls flew high above her, their faint screams fading in the wind. Ruth's spirit soared in the beauty of the natural world. She felt free.

Chapter 16

One beautiful day in April and the ocean was calm. Anthony woke Ruth.

"Let's go on a day trip." He suggested. There was a boyish enthusiasm in him, Ruth noticed. He rushed her through breakfast. He clearly was excited about something.

They headed to one of his boats, just the two of them and a picnic basket of food.

The trip was three hours out, heading north. The water remained calm, and the sun shone brightly down on the two. Ruth had to tie her hair back to combat the force of wind created by the speeding boat. Anthony was all grins. He steered the boat north, passing between Vancouver Island and the Interior. Once past the Old City, there were no human settlements to be seen — just land masses of tall evergreens. Ruth spotted Lodgepole pine, Douglas fir, and

Cedar. A couple of fishing ships were to the south. Soon Anthony and Ruth were out of sight from any other human, mort or halted.

A series of small islands, heavily forested, were visible between Vancouver Island and the interior. Anthony continued past two of islands; these were uninhabited. A third island appeared. Anthony steered up to the northern point and then circled it to approach it from the west. Before the halting, this area was sparsely populated. Now it seemed completely abandoned by any type of human settlement.

Anthony docked the boat at an ancient dock. They could not easily spot its well-hidden location during their approach. Ruth wondered how he found it, how he knew about this place.

"What is this place?" Ruth finally asked when she walked off the ancient wooden dock. Anthony just grinned and motioned for her to follow. He walked into the wood line, following an ancient gravel road, heavily grooved by rain and the seasons. The sun shone above in the cloudless sky, but the slight breeze was brisk.

"Anthony, come on." Ruth laughed. She judged based on his behaviour that this was a pleasant surprise, but she still wanted him to explain himself. Anthony's excitement was growing on her, and she felt inexplicitly lighthearted.

Anthony motioned for Ruth to follow him and they walked further down the road. Soon Ruth saw outbuildings nestled in the woods. It looked like several cabins and a main building. It must have been quite pretty centuries ago. Today, the buildings looked abandoned, forgotten by time.

"Anvil Island Lodge. I bought this old fishing resort decades ago. Few people know, except Rick and Mike." Anthony finally explained.

They walked around the cabins and the main house, the outbuildings. Ruth saw a couple of ancient trucks, rusted thoroughly and parked near the main house. A dilapidated sport boat leaning on one side was near an outbuilding. The signage for the lodge was so old and faded, most of it was now rotted flat boards or just the decayed stumps. Woods surrounding were vibrant in contrast, vivid green and heavily scented of pine and damp earth. The entire island was loud with the sound of birds and chattering critters, such as squirrels and chipmunks. Dragon flies flew swiftly around in the rays of the sun. A herd of tiny island deer scattered at the sight of Ruth and Anthony, causing a commotion as flights of birds swirled up to the cloudless sky.

"I wanted a place to move to, you know, if things go sideways. Part of me also thought maybe you and I could just live out here. Just you and me. Damn the world, damn everything."

Ruth thought about it, life here with Anthony, away from Blackmore and the halted, away from the morts, including Paul. No power struggles, no preparing for a threatening war, no fear of being in Alan Blackmore's captivity once more, no more being trapped and confined. It was a romantic dream, just the two of them playing house here in all this beauty. Maybe it would be safer here in the face of the upcoming war. But it seemed wrong somehow, a coward's way out. Ruth also knew it was not a very practical dream. She could not imagine Anthony living in the wilderness, away from the luxuries of his current life.

Anthony opened the door to the main house. It was once modern and sleek for the pre halt times — glass and steel. Now it was shabby under ancient dirt and dust. The windows were streaked with centuries of dirt. The floor had half an inch of forest debris dragged in, desiccated brown. Who knew what critters made nests in here? Then they took a few more steps, and it seemed that someone had swept the floor recently, maybe several months ago. Wooden boxes were piled everywhere. Anthony opened one for Ruth to peer in. Canned food and bottled water. Other boxes held cleaning and medical supplies.

"I have been stockpiling." Anthony laughed sheepishly. "I know. I am committed to fighting Blackmore, LIFETECH, and the Council, but I like to have a Plan B."

The main building had a wrap-around porch. Anthony grabbed a broom and swept a sunny patch clear. Ruth laid a blanket down. They sat to enjoy their picnic, a simple meal of bread, cheeses, and cured meats. There were fruit from Anthony's orchard, a bottle of wine, and Abigail's wonderful pastries.

"My father used to bring me here when I was a teenager. They rebuild the lodge and the cabins since then. It was a bit more rustic back then but still glamping, I guess."

Ruth puzzled over that word.

"Camping in luxury. I guess you never had that opportunity. My father rented a very nice cabin." Anthony motioned to where it once stood, replaced by another cabin over the centuries. "It had a beautiful fireplace that the staff would light for us each evening. We would fish or speed around the island on a boat. The staff would fry up what we caught, plus maybe some steaks. Dad would let me have a beer. We had wonderful times here."

"Oh Anthony, it does sound lovely. I remember my father took mom and me camping a couple of times before he died. Of course, it was in a tent — we were not wealthy. Hotdogs and marshmallows until I was nearly sick. I even caught a fish with him. I miss them. Hundreds of years later, I miss my mom and dad."

Anthony nodded in agreement. They both were silent for a moment.

"Well, what do you think? Run away and live here with me?" he broached the subject again. "Honestly, Ruth, that was my first thought when I bought the property. Even back then, I wanted out, and I wanted to bring you with me."

Ruth did not respond. She reached for his hand, trying to understand how she felt. If only he had offered this — a life on this island — a century ago. She felt though an obligation now to Paul and Anne, and, as she got to know the people in Anthony's compound, she felt that obligation extend to include them.

"I know. We got to see the plan through. I owe that to many, many people, especially you." Anthony sighed heavily.

They ate slowly, appreciating the beauty of this abandoned resort and the mild warmth of the spring sun. After they tidied up, placing the blanket and the reminder of the food in the basket neatly. They moved slowly, as if they could drag out the moment.

"I have something else to show you." Anthony led Ruth to one of the cabins near where the old cabin of Antony's youth was. It was in the best condition of the group of cabins. Like the other buildings, it was dusty and dirty. Ruth spotted a cracked window, but when Anthony opened the door, the rooms and furniture were intact. The dust was not as thick as in the main building: he had taken care of this particular cabin. More boxes of supplies were stacked in the kitchen area.

Anthony motioned to the larger bedroom; his eyebrow arched questioningly. Ruth laughed and followed him.

Afterwards, Ruth laid her head on his bare chest, the picnic blanket covering them from the chill that permeated the musty room.

"Anthony, why did you agree to be halted?" Ruth asked a question she had for centuries.

"I don't even know why myself. I guess, at first, I didn't really think it would really work. Maybe I would just gain some extra time, maybe keep arthritis and whatever old age ailments at bay for a while. Stall dementia. I saw my father whither away, you know, from Alzheimer's. All my life he was a strong, vibrant man, sharp mind, and then he could barely dress himself and didn't know who he was, didn't even know me. Halting was going to stop that from happening to me and others. Ruth, I honestly thought LIFETECH was a pioneer in creating a better world.

Eventually, it would share the wealth, and everyone would benefit. Stupid. Stupid. I just sat there and let this all happen. I let them and the others keep the rest of the world down. Probably because I didn't want to fail. All my life I've been on top. Best schools, great job, controlling the shots. I was afraid, afraid of losing my place. If I stayed with LIFETECH, I had some control, I thought. I was weak. I still am weak. I can't blame you if you hate me."

Chapter 17

It was May and the aging virus was ready. Successful testing occurred on a couple of halted volunteers in a compound out east. The halted resistance had grown to thousands of persons since last summer, Anthony explained to Ruth. Halted were willing to leave their cocoons of privilege for similar reasons — they were tired of a shallow existence, the monotony, the boredom where nothing progressed. Several halted volunteered to test the virus themselves, willing to risk death to return to their natural state of aging. The researchers chose two of the halted volunteers and administered the virus to them. After mild flu-like symptoms, they appeared to be in normal health. A month later and their examinations indicated the restart of cellular aging. The two halted appeared to resume normal aging after a long pause. The digi-medics would not detect the changes for several months.

Pleased with the initial success, the halted group of the resistance decided to expand testing. They had no issues with finding willing participants. Hundreds of halted across North America were injected willingly.

Questions arose about how to infect the larger halted communities. The quickest way was to infect the water supply, but it would involve significant quantities of the virus. Affecting the food source seemed more achievable. Testing expanded to morts and animals. The virus was adjusted to ensure it would not harm them. Paul volunteered to test the virus, and Ruth waited anxiously for the news of the outcome. She nearly cried with relief to hear Paul had minor flu-like symptoms and no sign of any effects on his cellular aging.

The virus was replicated and smuggled to major farming centres that grew leafy green produce such as lettuce and sprouts throughout North America and South America and parts of Europe, focusing on the major areas that produced vegetables for the halted. Most morts could not afford this produce and grew their own produce in community gardens or purchase canned vegetables. It was the morts that laboured on these farms, producing food for the halted that they couldn't afford. Now the morts smuggled the virus in and infected the produce that fed the halted.

The council of the corporations had to be weakened, too. Mort resistance cells would address this part of the plan by attacking key infrastructure and the various corporation headquarters with a variety of EMP bombs and conventional incendiary bombs. This was to occur shortly after the virus release.

The release of the virus coincided with the opening of the summer party circuit. Anthony had laid low for nearly a year with Ruth. Now he felt he needed to be seen out and about in order to draw attention away from his compound.

He began to RSVP to some of the smaller parties. Ruth urged him to let her attend with him. Ruth was nervous, but she felt she could not let Anthony go alone. He was taking an enormous risk; the virus was released a week ago and slowly affecting the halted communities. Mild flu-like symptoms were prevalent on the halted compounds. It was highly contagious, an unexpected result which aided the resistance groups. They could let nature do its job once they released it into the environment. Anthony though wanted to confirm that key people were infected and to ensure the digi-medics were not detecting the changes. Ruth suspected he was also curious and wanted to witness a potentially watershed moment up close.

The first couple of parties were relatively uneventful. The first was a yacht party down south that gathered a small group of relatively minor players in the halted world. The second was an equestrian event, featuring horse jumping and a rowdy polo match in the evening. At both events, Ruth and Anthony avoided most of the LIFETECH group.

The third one was the annual party at Alan Blackmore's compound. Ruth and Anthony planned to go. Or so Ruth thought. She had seen little of Anthony during the days leading up to the party. He was away on business for several days, meeting with the lead corporations in their area. Anthony wanted to be out in the open while checking on the progress of the local resistance cells clandestinely. He still had to earn an income too, though he was slowly divesting his properties in order to stockpile supplies and money.

Ruth found she missed Anthony dearly. It was the longest period they had been apart since last summer. She was excited to see him when he finally arrived home the day before. He arrived late and immediately pleaded he was exhausted; Ruth could see that with her own eyes. Anthony had dark circles around his eyes, and he stooped forward as if he was shouldering a colossal weight. It was the first night in quite a while that they did not share a bed while they were both under the same roof.

Ruth paced the room that night. Alan Blackmore was at the equestrian party two weeks ago, but Ruth and Anthony successfully avoided him in the sizeable crowd of attention seeking party goers. Ruth did manage to see Melissa Hammel. They bumped into each other in the women's washroom, of all places. Melissa was as glittery and sparkling as she remembered. They exchanged pleasantries. Of course, Melissa looked Ruth up and down, seeking information.

"You look well, Ruth." Melissa concluded. Melissa, on closer inspection, looked weary. Her eyes drooped under the heavy layers of face paint and glitter.

"Are you well, Melissa? Are they treating you well?" Ruth inquired in a low voice. Melissa shrugged. With no other topics to keep the small talk going, Melissa walked away. Ruth heard Melissa's hard laugh moments later as the younger woman greeted a group of others in the corridor.

This night, alone in her bed without Anthony, Ruth had a series of disturbing dreams. The most vivid one was of Anthony. They were back on Anvil Island, talking on the veranda of the main building. Then Anthony appeared to be ill. No, he was aging rapidly, like time sped up a hundred-fold. His hair was thin and grey, his face tired and wrinkled. His fleeting mortality struck Ruth hard. In this dream, she remained changed, still halted. Forever stuck at age thirty when even Anthony aged.

An old woman then stepped into her dream. She was ancient, with patchy white hair on her fragile head and large liver spots on her ancient face and hands. She reached out and grabbed Ruth's arm, youthful and smooth. *Mom, it's Molly. Where have you been, Mom? Where did you go?* The old woman held Ruth's arm, her yellowed nails dug into Ruth's smooth arm. Ruth woke, heart pounding.

Chapter 18

Ruth finally met up with Anthony the next day. She was anxious and felt compelled several times to knock on his door, demanding to see him. Ruth though waited instead for him to seek her out. She still felt uneasy about the lack of contact from him since he arrived. She wondered if he intentionally refrained from any physical contact last night. The old insecurities plagued her as she questioned his feelings for her and wondered if he already was pulling away from her. So, when Anthony finally joined Ruth on the balcony that afternoon, dressed for the party, she was immensely relieved. His outfit, as usual, complemented his form; he always looked younger than his halted age of forty-eight. Anthony hugged Ruth, sincere in his pleasure to be with her. Her fears over the last twenty-four hours melted away.

"Well, what will you be wearing tonight? Polyester suit?" Anthony gently teased. His comment reminded Ruth it had been a year since Alan's last party, when she was paraded around in that dated outfit. She laughed.

"Something fancier, I hope. Anthony, it would be nice to never see his face again."

"I know, I know. But we should keep up appearances for a little longer. The longer the halted resistance is left unnoticed, the better chance we have of making a genuine change." Anthony kissed her hand. "You don't have to come. I don't want to put you in his grasp."

"No, I need to do something. I don't think I could stand it, knowing you are there alone. Anyway, I do know unarmed combat." Ruth replied. Anthony graciously laughed at her small joke.

Ruth dressed for the party in a beautiful dress of emerald green; the fabric felt delicious on her skin. They arrived at the Blackmore's compound. As they left Anthony's vehicle, Ruth felt fortified with Anthony's warm, firm hand on the small of her back. Ruth allowed herself to lean against him and they walked up the front entrance and moved through the old familiar great wood door. The door was massive, constructed from red oak and decorated with etched lines and swirls, imitating the long past art décor era. Ruth wondered how many times she walked through this door to start one of her runs. Ruth recognized some of the mort staff tasked to greet the guests and usher them to the great hall. She walked past the security booth, still leaning against Anthony's arm. As in the past, the morts at Blackmore Compound avoided eye contact with her.

This year's theme was fire and ice. A lot of the entertainment involved fire acts: jugglers with fire sticks, fire eaters, dancers with ropes lit on fire. Elaborate ice sculptures decorated the great hall and garden grounds. The temperature in the room was cool; Ruth shivered in the silky fabric of her gown. Many of the guests wrapped themselves in white fur shawls provided by the Blackmore Compound. Ruth suspected Alan's latest obsession over the last decade — hunting — provided all the furs. Instead of utilizing the furs, Ruth and Anthony headed to the garden grounds where fire installations projected rapid moving shadows.

The evening air, in contrast to the great hall, was warm and the heat from the fire installations added to it. Anthony slipped out of his jacket and swung it over his shoulder with the graceful ease he possessed naturally. They accepted champaign flutes from the serving staff and sipped, making more of a show of drinking rather than actually consuming. They had to keep their wits about them. This was really no different from the numerous other times when Ruth has been in Alan's vicinity.

They skirted the long banquet tables of food. Ruth saw delicacies from all over the globe artfully laid out — seafood, rare beef, caviar. The others, like Alan Blackmore, served up a ridiculously extravagant spread to signal that they were the dominant entities on this planet. Many of the dishes were from nearly extinct species such as polar bear and sea turtle. The chefs garnished most of the dishes with greens such as kale, lettuce, and other leafy produce — Ruth suspected all these greens were harvested from the industrial farms which were contaminated with the virus. The resistance groups had fully infiltrated all the area farms weeks ago and released the virus into the farms' water supply. All this vegetation grew in the affected water. The runoff from the industrial farms by now had moved into the streams and rivers; soon, most water supplies, if not all, would be contaminated. Ruth watched with fascination as the others ate the food, unaware.

Ruth and Anthony were in the garden for over an hour when they saw Alan Blackmore enter with Rob McDonald, Maury Poirrier, Melissa Hammel, and other lower-level others trailing behind. Alan wore his customary whites. Now that he was outside, away from the ice sculptures, Alan took off a white fur and handed it to Melissa. The pristine fur was a dazzling white; arctic fox, Ruth guessed. Melissa draped the fur over her forearm.

"I see you have not grown tired of the little mouse. Yet." Alan smirked as he passed by Anthony and Ruth. The encounter to outsiders looked accidental, but Ruth knew it was intentional. Alan hated the two of them and he could not give up an opportunity to lord over them while he tried to determine their intentions.

Anthony just smiled and kissed Ruth's hand. Alan scowled. Ruth looked into Anthony's face, attempting to look like she was fawning over him. And if she was honest with herself, she did not have to fake it. Her feelings were strong for him. He was not Marco, but he was kind and loving, and she had grown to trust him. As Ruth looked up at Anthony, she noticed Anthony's eyes were a touch bleary and his hair near his forehead was damp.

"Her rooms are empty, regardless, for when you want to return her, though I may not be interested for long in accepting her back. Perhaps we will be both tired of her." Alan made one last barb and continued to lead his entourage through the crowds. Melissa squeezed Ruth's hand as she passed, a furtive action hidden from the others. Ruth felt the sensation of fur caressing her arm. Melissa looked like she wanted to say something to Ruth. Hopefully Ruth will get a moment alone with Melissa later.

While Anthony and Ruth were attending the party, Paul Foster and a small group of morts from his resistant group were in the Blackmore compound, too. Paul maintained his network within the compound, which provided the two groups, Anthony's and Paul's, with intelligence. Tonight, Paul's group were to sabotage the digi-medics so it would not detect the virus. The virus was not only on the tables of food, but on the silver trays, hidden in the prepared foods, working its way throughout the party. Ruth politely declined when a stoney face mort presented the platter of appetizers to her. Ruth imagined that by now most of the produce in North America was infected. Halted were coming down with mysterious, seemingly insignificant colds or flus throughout North America; the media reported yesterday, noting the uptake in colds and flus. Ruth knew the Resistant teams were working now on spreading the virus to the other continents.

The next stage would be the dismantling the council of the corporations, Ruth mused. The mort resistance, funded and supplied by sympathetic others like Anthony, would increase their acts of rebellion and try to destroy the major corporations and their facilities. Ruth considered the possibility of her and Anthony being compelled to fight in an actual armed conflict. Perhaps they would assume a more active role in the impending war. She wondered what those roles would be. The image of her carrying arms still seemed utterly ridiculous.

Having made their appearance to the halted community and, Ruth and Anthony decided to leave the party. There was no point in pressing their luck.

At the front entrance, security stopped them.

"What is the meaning of this?" Anthony demanded. Guards were on both sides of Ruth and Anthony, holding firmly to their arms. Ruth and Anthony were forced into the lift, up to the offices. Then they were pushed into a small conference room. Anthony's own security team was nowhere in sight.

Ruth and Anthony were held in the room for hours. It must have been well past midnight when the door opened in and in walked Alan Blackmore, with Rob McDonald and Maury Poirrier trailing behind.

Anthony repeated his question. He attempted to walk up to Alan, but a security guard shoved him back.

"Sit down, both of you." Alan ordered. The last thing Ruth wanted to do was obey him, but she saw Anthony sit as ordered. She sat too, hoping to resolve whatever the situation was. Did Blackmore security catch Paul or one of his group lurking in a room they should not be? The thought terrified her.

"Mr. Gelinas, there have been rumours. Rumours of halted members colluding with morts, perhaps even arming the morts."

"Are you accusing me of something?"

"I never pegged you as a bleeding-heart idealist, Anthony. I assume she nudged you towards that way, but I can't see how. I don't see the appeal." Alan turned to Ruth, hissing venom, "you stupid nobody, you should have died back then. Stupid, stupid little mouse. And you, writing garbage for the morts. It humoured us. The council had quite a few laughs. You are nothing, a nobody. I kept you around to remind you of that. You are nothing, just like that stupid spouse of yours who got himself killed."

Ruth lunged at Alan, catching him unaware. She ran her fist into his throat. He fell back, coughing, clutching his throat. A guard grabbed her and hit her hard across the head with a baton. She fell into the chair, then struggled to sit up, her dress torn near the collar. Rob and Maury quickly moved back from her, well behind Allan Blackmore. Anthony moved towards her as if he could try to shield her. The guard shoved him down. Ruth smiled, knowing she hurt Alan. She trained decades for that chance, she realised, to make him hurt, if only a little. She finally had that moment.

"I will not entertain your accusations, Alan, and you will regret it if anyone hurts Ruth." Anthony spat his words at Alan. Ruth had every confidence that Anthony would not betray a single member, mort or halted, of the resistance. Alan could not fully comprehend, as she saw it; Ruth and Anthony had nothing to lose. Anthony was just as tired of this meaningless existence as she was. He wanted a fight. Then Ruth was struck with the realization of how badly she wanted a fight, too.

Alan motioned to the security guard, and the guard swung the baton across Anthony's head. Anthony's body recoiled and blood gathered on his temple, dripping on to his shirt. Ruth screamed and was hit again by the same guard. She fought through the pain and lunged at the guard, clawing at his face. More guards came in to subdue her. Alan and his party backed away and tried to leave the room, but a large crashing sound startled them all. More strange sounds followed, muffled through the wall. Something sounded like gunshots, followed by people screaming. Outside the conference door, the noise grew. Whatever was happening was moving closer to the office. People scuffled in the hall, crying and shouting. Alan ordered security to check it out.

"Sir, intruders. You should come with us." One of the Blackmore guards returned within minutes, panting hard, his weapon ready in his hand. Soon Ruth and Anthony were alone in the room. It was locked, though. They were trapped. Gun shots rang out.

"What is going on, Anthony?" Ruth asked as she stood up to check him over. A large bruise was forming on his temple, turning an angry purple. Ruth felt her own head, her ear was wet with blood.

"I have no idea. Maybe Paul was discovered, and he's fighting back." Anthony cupped her face with one hand and moved her bloodied hair from her face. "Alan has always been a fool. Not as smart as he thinks he is. Far from it. He does not know how valuable you are. Took me a while though to fully realize it myself."

"Oh, Anthony, this is terrible timing," she murmured. His forehead was glistening with sweat and blood; a large welt on his forehead was forming, and she touched it gingerly. His skin was hot. She noticed he looked was feverish. "What is going on? Are you ill?"

He smiled sheepishly. "I wanted this. The virus. I want to move on and join the humans again. I know I should have said something to you. Honestly, I think you understand. You want the virus too. I thought somehow I should test it first."

She nodded and kissed him. Another gun shot rang out.

"I hope you are contagious." Ruth laughed nervously.

The commotion outside their room continued. They both searched the room for a key, a way out. Anthony tried running his shoulder into the door, but they were trapped. The smell of smoke seeped into the room. There were no windows in the room to give any hint of what was happening.

Finally, a knock at the door and then a jiggling of keys. The door swung open, and it was a security guard. Paul stepped in from behind him. This security guard was one of Paul's people, Ruth deduced, but she did not recognize him from the planning sessions at Anthony's compound.

"What is going on?" Anthony demanded. Ruth was relieved, though, to see Paul alive and well.

"Anthony, I know you are not going to like this. It's not the plan, well, your plan. But we took overtook the compound. The morts working here and my group. The group here was itching for a coup; they had a plan for tonight. I thought the opportunity was too tempting."

"Bloody hell, Paul!"

"Well, it might have worked to your advantage. I heard Blackmore planned to seize you two tonight and hold you in his cells. He planned to strong-arm the Council in trying you for treason. They would have tortured you to get names. My name and the names of my colleagues. I didn't want that to happen."

"What are they doing?" Ruth asked. With the door open, she could see smoke drifting in the halls. The screams and commotion were loud and frantic.

"My group is rounding up the guests." Paul added a sarcastic tone to the word guests. "Some will be ransomed, but I fear Mr. Blackmore and his group will be executed on the spot if they are found. My people are too angry to leave him to chance. I'd like him to be captured alive, but I don't know if that is possible. You two need to leave now. Ruth, you know where you should go."

Paul led them down the emergency stairs. He gave Ruth a bag of mort clothes to change into later. Paul clearly prepared for this. They got to the main floor and Paul acted as if they were his hostages. Ruth saw morts with guns surrounding a large group of frighten and confused halted partiers, their outrageous outfits ripped and bloodied. A body of a woman laid by the coatroom, blood pooling underneath her. Another body leaned slumped against the wall before the great hall. Ruth had foolishly hoped it would be a bloodless revolution, but she also felt the centuries of injustice burned hot, even for herself. She realized, when she lunged at Allan up in that room, she would have killed him herself if she could.

Ruth spotted Melissa Hammel huddled in the group.

"Paul, I want that woman to join us."

Paul stared at Ruth, reluctant to comprehend.

"Please, she was coerced into Blackmore's group when she was a teenager. She was barely an adult."

Paul nodded and moved them closer to the halted group.

Ruth grabbed Melissa's arm. "Don't say a word. You need to come with us now if you want to survive this."

Melissa held on to Ruth's hand tight, whimpering. She looked like a raccoon; her makeup smeared, running down her face, mixed with snot and tears.

Once outside the house, Paul got them outside the gate through a hole in the fence he created days ago. Thick bushes hid it from security.

"Security was obviously not that loyal to Blackmore to be motivated to examine the fence line properly," said Paul.

He said his goodbyes and headed back to the house. Ruth was in charge now. She checked the bag and found a collection of work pants, shirts, and shoes. Paul fortunately had a variety of sizes. Nothing really fit properly, but it hid their fancy outfits, and the shoes were better than the flimsy heels both women were wearing.

Once dressed, the three headed to the woods. Ruth knew the way by heart, even in the dark. Melissa, ever the survivor, wiped her smeared make up partially off with one hand and took a few long calming breaths. She marched behind Ruth. Anthony followed silently behind. His head lowered with dejection. He likely felt very betrayed by Paul and his group, but Ruth had no time to dwell on it. She quickly moved into the woods and motioned for the others to follow.

The three made it to the creek. Each took the time to wash their bloodied, dirty faces and hands. The cool water was soothing. Moonlight slipped between the trees and reflected silver on the running creek water. They also drank greedily the creek water, using their hands as cups. All they could do now was wait. Ruth hope Paul would come get them. Surely, he had not betrayed them. She was his great grandmother, six times great after all, she mused. She strangely had faith in Paul. He would come. They would not be abandoned.

All three were exhausted and tried to make themselves comfortable under the tree where Ruth first saw Paul here. They used the extra clothes for warmth as a chill set in. Melissa was visibly shaking, even though she still had Alan's fur with her. Probably shock, Ruth reasoned.

Anthony's illness progressed, and he looked so tired and old. It was startling to see him this way. He looked similar to the Anthony in Ruth's nightmare. She feared for a moment that the virus did not just start his aging clock, but it was rapidly aging him — too quickly. Was there a problem with the virus?

Ruth insisted Anthony lay his head on her lap, and she wrapped her arms around him. Ruth herself felt exhausted, starving, and cold. Huddled into Anthony, she slept fitfully. Her body ached, exasperated from sitting on the cold, damp forest floor. Her left hip throbbed.

Daylight started to seep into the woods and the birdsong grew louder, as did as the chatter of small animals. Anthony stirred in her lap, coughing. His forehead was still hot and damp, perhaps worse now. He gingerly sat up with Ruth's help. Melissa was sitting cross-legged nearby, the dirty fur wrapped around her shoulders. Melissa looked like a child, scared and uncertain. The hard look she usually held was gone. What now, both Anthony and Melissa seemed to ask Ruth silently. She had no answer, so she remained quiet.

Branches rustled from the other side of the creek, the side closer to the mort settlement. All three sat straighter, alert.

"Ruth, it's Anne. Ruth," the shaky voice of an older woman was heard. Three shapes came closer. One supported the shorter figure of the old woman, armed tucked under hers.

Ruth jumped up to her feet and rushed over.

"Anne, I am so happy to see you." Ruth reached out for the older woman, embracing her firmly. "Is it safe for you to come here, though?"

"You mean because of my age?" Anne chuckled. She was with her two grandchildren, whom she introduced as Josie and Ryan. Both morts stared long and hard at Ruth and Ruth realized these two were also descendants of her and Marco. She smiled warmly at them.

"You three look a bit rough around the edges. We need to move you, though. There is a cottage near the settlement. Can you walk?" Josie, the older grandchild, spoke. She looked at Anthony, who was slummed on the ground, looking fragile.

Ruth helped Anthony to his feet. He was quite ill, but confirmed he was ambulatory. Melissa trailed behind, close to Ruth.

The cottage was rustic by even mort standards. It was an old forgotten hunting cabin. Anne's family had left some supplies — canned food, water, basic first aid kit. Josie and Ryan got working on lighting up the wood stove to boil water for drinking and heat up food. Anne checked over the three for injuries and did her best to clean up the head wounds. She clucked over Anthony, noticing he had a fever. Anne then turned her attention to Melissa.

"Where are you from?" the old lady asked Melissa.

"From Chilliwack, east of here. My family was the Hammels. I haven't been there in fifty years," Melissa said. Fifty years since Melissa was halted — left unsaid but clearly understood.

"Were your people Joanne and James?" Anne asked

"James was my brother." Melissa replied, her voice broke with emotion.

"Is your brother. He is still alive, in his seventies. Sound right? He married my cousin Joanne. They are still in Chilliwack."

Melissa was speechless for quite a while, staring at Anne with wet eyes.

The three — Ruth, Anthony and Melissa — were fed and put into bunk beds in a backroom under Anne's direction. Ruth curled up against Anthony's back on the bottom bunk, her arms holding him as if he might fall out of bed.

"Get a room, you two," she heard Melissa quip from the other side. Melissa sounded stronger, less afraid. Ruth laughed in response. Melissa and Anthony joined in, and the laughter grew. It became more about the relief of tension rather than a bad old joke. It then set Anthony into a coughing fit. His eyes were grateful, though, when Ruth fussed over him.

Chapter 19

Ruth, Anthony, and Melissa spend a couple of weeks in that cottage. Anne's family brought supplies over daily, as well as news. The revolt, it was what they referred the events at the Blackmore compound to, settled on a temporary resolution. Alan, Maury, and Rob were apprehended at the compound airstrip. The morts also apprehended key council members who were present at the party. All put in an ancient county jail on the outskirts of the old city of Vancouver. Many of the minor level halted were ransomed off. Quite a few of them were forced to pay their own ransom as they had no family or close acquaintances.

Anthony had two rough days, then he began to recover. Ruth, then Melissa, became ill. It was short-lived, fortunately. Ruth explained to Melissa about the virus and its effects the first morning at the cabin as Anthony slept fitfully. Ruth was surprised that Melissa's reaction was one of immense relief.

"Thank god." Melissa said after a period of reflection, "Maybe I will finally wake from this nightmare."

Revolts such as the revolt at Blackmore compound happened all over North America and, in several places, such as the European Union and the United Kingdom, much further than Anthony predicted. Stories of a mysterious illness that plagued the halted grew; Paul heard the virus had reached far into Europe.

More members of the council were taken into custody. In the east, the revolts grew ugly, and many halted were publicly executed, often hung. Their corpses were left hanging in halted communities.

The stories of that mystery virus continued to increase. The virus was beyond the Americas and Europe; it was everywhere now, even into Africa and Asia. It remained highly contagious. Mostly, the virus and its symptoms were mild, though some halted persons died. It hit the mort community but with fewer symptoms. Ruth learnt Anne had gotten it and she had several anxious days until she received word that Anne recovered.

On the fifteenth day, Paul came to the cottage.

"Alan Blackmore and his staff were sick, but now recovered. It hit them hard, but they are alive. Blackmore is offering a lot of money for his own release. He is lucky he is alive. We have a lot of security on him, mainly to keep him alive. His own people want him dead. The Council wants him dead. Us morts especially want him dead." Paul shared the latest news over cups of tea and bowls of canned soup.

"Is there anything left of the Council?" Anthony asked.

"Bits and pieces, mostly out of the African and Asian areas. The Council is barely existing though, losing Europe and the Americas. I fear they will close the circle and protect what they have left in Asia and Africa. The Council still have footholds in Australia and New Zealand too. The virus hasn't impacted that far out — yet."

"What about us? Paul?" Melissa interrupted, "No offence, Ruth, but I can't stay here, shacked up with the love birds like I am their moody teen or some kind of third wheel. I can't live indefinitely in this cabin."

"What would you do? Where would you go?" Paul looked at Melissa, curious. Melissa could not answer; she left her home and family decades ago, abandoning the mort community for what she had hoped was a better life. Regret shaped her expression.

"What about Ruth and myself?" Anthony asked. "Are we free to go back to my compound? What about the others in my group? Mike, Rick, everyone at my compound?"

Anthony broached a difficult subject. The men grew tense. Paul shifted in his chair.

"I can appreciate your situation, Anthony, I really do. The tables are turning on you. I also appreciate your support. We wouldn't have gotten to Blackmore and LIFETECH without your assistance, your resources, but I have little control here though. The mort community is angry, centuries of repression and injustice. I can't control my own people. I am though working on amnesty for you and your group. If you could lie low for a while, then we could work towards the coalition of our two peoples like we talked about. The mort community knows it needs your access to knowledge, your resources. I am certain we can come to favourable terms."

Day eighteen, Paul escorted the three to Anthony's compound. Anthony's mort staff had made several changes and made themselves at home. This beautiful place no longer belonged to Anthony. Most of them refused to look Anthony and Ruth in the eyes. Few of the morts wore expressions of guilt, as if pleading to Anthony for his understanding.

Paul had brokered an agreement. Anthony and Ruth had a week to pack up items such as clothes and supplies and load them on the boats, the ones Anthony and his group could manoeuvre on their own. His smaller yachts were the obvious choice; ones he could operate without a large crew. Anthony also planned to bring as much of his book collection and datapads that he could.

"Well, come on Melissa, looks like you are shopping in my wardrobe." Ruth made light of the situation. She had insisted that Melissa join Anthony and her at Anvil Island and stay until Melissa had a plan of her own.

Anthony was quiet, defeated by the swiftness of his staff's change of allegiance. Ruth knew he would have to figure it out himself that even though he gradually grew to be sympathetic to their plight, he still exploited the morts, including his mort staff. He couldn't expect their undying loyalty to continue in this new world that was emerging.

"Looks like I get to continue being third wheel." Melissa said in a light tone.

Packing clothing with Melissa was unexpectedly fun. Melissa teased Ruth about her clothing options.

"Dull, Dull. Drab. Boring." Melissa pronounced.

Ruth had not laughed like that in centuries.

Ruth and Melissa made lists of items they would need: winter gear, rain gear, linens. For how long? Ruth had to ask for Paul's help to get extra items, such as a variety of outer wear. She was afraid to ask Anthony's former mort staff. Few of them acknowledged her or any of the halted.

Packing books and supplies with Anthony was serious work. He agonized over each item as he could not take everything with him, and he feared the morts would not value the ones left behind. He worried that they would leave the books vulnerable to the elements, away from the environmental controls of his library. Many items in his book and manuscript collections were centuries older than him.

Anthony was able to contact and collect all of his group, the local sympathetic halted who worked with him over the year -- the ones Ruth trained with last fall. All were now former halted. This group, Anthony's group, as Ruth thought of them as, agreed to come with Anthony to Anvil Island. With Melissa, that made twelve of them, destinated for Anvil Island. No morts offered to join Anthony or to assist his exodus, not even John Reilly or Abigail Wise, whom Anthony particularly favoured. Ruth, Melissa, and Anthony's group organized and loaded three of Anthony's boats by themselves. Rick and Mike arrived at the compound days prior to departure, with bags and boxes of hastily packed items from Anthony's other properties.

By now the halted community had learnt of the virus. Most of the community suffered from its infection themselves, recovered, and now resumed aging. True immortals were far and few now. Instead of an outcry, a significant sized population of former halted seemed to share the sense of relief. They seemed to recognize they were frozen in time. People need change. They need to evolve.

"We were always living on borrowed time, at the expense of our humanity. Of course it is a relief." Anthony remarked to Ruth.

Despite the general relief from immortality from some, many of the former halted were devastated to lose their status and the wealth that accompanied it, but there was no going back. The mort resistance destroyed all LIFETECH business properties; they destroyed company servers and files, including files holding the secrets to halting. LIFETECH, in its bid to remain on top, had refused to share its secret to halting aging. Its secret died in the servers near the old city. It was unlikely Rob McDonald or Maury Poirrier, or any of the others involved in engineering the process for immortality, would be able to piece together this secret after two hundred and fifty years. Not for a very long time. The halted community had failed to advance the science. They barely maintained scientific advances from the prehalt.

Paul appeared the day of departure. He told them of the plans to put Alan Blackmore and the other key council members on trial.

"What will happen if they find us guilty?" Anthony asked warily. This new world was confusing to him, shifting in ways he did not predict. Ruth could not help but to feel pity for him, despite the choices he made hundreds of years ago.

"I don't know, my friend," Paul spoke sympathetically, "Go and lie low for a while."

To Ruth, Paul handed a package, in addition to the supplies she requested.

"From Anne. She wanted to give this to you herself, but she is feeling under the weather today. Nothing to worry about,

Ruth. Anne is fine. Just the usual ailments of old age. You will experience it yourself soon enough, I expect."

Inside a brown paper bag, there were smaller bags of seeds and plant clippings, carefully labelled in a shaky hand. A roll of paper held by an elastic band. Ruth removed the band as Paul grinned widely. It was a stack of paper, old and yellowed, in Ruth's own hand. Something she copied out decades ago and left to chance in one of her hiding holes — a book on gardening.

"How can you even read that?" Melissa noted as she examined the words on the yellowed pages, "It looks like a child's scribbles."

The journey was over three hours by water and Anthony led the way. The other two boats followed, a solemn convoy up the peninsula. The mood was a stark contrast to the mood of last spring when Anthony brought Ruth to the Island. This day, the sun was fierce in the hot summer sky.

Seagulls screeched above them as Anthony led the small convoy to Anvil Island. They docked the boats and started the hard work of unloading. The sun slowly set as they worked: many of them never had to lift much in the last centuries, especially their own suitcases. They struggled with the physical task but did not complain out loud. The sky gradually shifted from pink to purple to dark indigo as the yellow orb of the sun dipped behind the blue horizon.

Chapter 20

In the morning's light, Ruth saw the lodge and the cabins were as she recalled, weathered and deserted near the middle of the small island. Anvil Lodge consisted of a main house with six bedrooms, five smaller cabins, and several outbuildings. A freshwater stream ran long the south side. Anthony laid claim the night before to the cabin he and Ruth spent that pleasant afternoon in April and let the others decide their own sleeping arrangements. In the main house, proof of Anthony's foresight was clear. Behind the boxes of supplies that Ruth noted on the first visit, there were solar panels, months and months supplies of dried and canned food and other crucial staples, water purifiers and batteries of every size and shape, a portal medical suite and various medical supplies. There was even a portable digi-medic.

Anthony purchased and collected every type of tool and gadget. In the outbuildings, there were hundreds of jerry cans of fuel, fishing and hunting equipment, and guns and ammo, locked in steel cabinets. It was now clear to everyone that Anthony had been working on this for decades, with only the involvement of Mike and Rick. They had brought over even more boxes over since that day trip in April. Everything was dusty but useable. If they were careful, the group could last a couple of years on the supplies.

The first week was spent cleaning the cabins and the main house. Everything had to be aired out and washed down. Ruth was the chief advisor on this. She had to fight the urge to roll her eyes up at the lack of life experience most of the group had. Most came from privileged backgrounds, involving housekeepers and chauffeurs. Melissa supported Ruth, ensuring the others followed Ruth's instructions as they tidied the buildings for habitation. Melissa did not flinch or squeal like the others in cleaning up the remnants of mice and other critters. She had retained vivid memories of her own youth as a mort living in poverty.

There was limited running water in the buildings — enough to flush the toilets and fill the sinks for basic washing. An ancient well was on the site and filling buckets of water for daily use became a communal chore, just like chopping wood and security patrols around the island. Rain barrels were positioned to catch rain water.

"Farewell to long hot showers." Dale Platonov grumbled. Ruth cringed a bit, reluctant to admit to herself how she missed the luxury of hot running water after only a couple of days on the island.

Rick and Mike hauled out the solar panels and generators. Cursing and sweating, they struggled to set up a mini power grid. By day three, they were able to provide basic light and electricity to operate the crucial kitchen appliances and the portable medical suite. They also were able to charge the datapads and the boat batteries. Cheers interrupted through the group the first time Mike and Rick were able to brew a decent pot of coffee. Hot water was, though still limited, achievable.

Alexandra Chen, the closest member of the Anvil Island to having a background in medicine, was tasked to learn how to operate the medical suite. She was a biologist at LIFETECH and had the closest experience to actual medical training. She set the medical suite with the dig-medic up in the main house. Her first patient was Dale Platonov. On the fourth day on Anvil Island, he crushed his finger chopping wood. It caused quite the commotion. Most of the group grew instantly pale at the sight of the bleeding finger. The skin was broken and the finger quickly ballooned up. Alexandra gulped but adopted a professional air and enlisted Mike and Rick's help in figuring out the portable x-ray scanned. Afterwards, Alexandra's face revealed clearly how proud she was of her actions. Dale spent the day in the big house, icing his tender swollen hand.

The cabin Anthony selected was beautiful after a proper cleaning, with two bedrooms. The living room had a fireplace and lots of shelving for books. The kitchen was small but had everything, assuming the electricity was consistent. The decent size refrigerator was not operational, but they hoped to get a solar panel working to fix that in the upcoming months.

The bedrooms too were beautiful once the musty, damp smell was gone and clean linens covered the beds. The cabin had a wrap-around deck with Adirondack chairs near the front door. Anthony probably never lived in something so modest, but for Ruth, it was a dream. Marco and Ruth could never had afforded to even rent such a place for even one night during a vacation. The cabin was also much larger than their old apartment. The only downsize was the limited water and electrical power. Ruth expected it also will be quite chilly in the winter without electric heat, but that was a concern for later.

Melissa set up shop in the cabin beside them. It had two bedrooms too, but Melissa put her foot down and scared off any roommates as she claimed the building as her own.

The next weeks were busy. Everything had to be inventoried and a strict food plan had to be developed to ensure they made it through to next June. Ideally, they wanted to stretch the current food stores into a second or third year. Who knew what the future held for them? Melissa proved to be a tremendous asset here; she was assertive, organized, and not afraid able to put the others in their place.

Ruth took control of two fitter looking members of the group and put them to work with her. They dug out an ancient garden plot near the main house and planted some quick growing plants to supplement the seemingly endless cans of food and bags of rice and other grains. A small apple orchard and berry bushes were discovered, overgrown and almost unreachable because of the overgrown bush. Ruth had her crew clear that out too and the Anvil Island group ate berries and apples until they were nearly sick of them. Apples were gathered and stored in the main house pantry and Ruth experimented with drying out the fruit for long-term storage. She also planned to experience with canning.

Wood also had to be collected to heat the buildings. The group cut up and dried deadfall for the winter months.

Anthony dug out an old ham radio and experimented with it. He had made arrangements with Paul Foster to keep in regular contact. With the radio, Anthony could make frequent, if not daily, contact with Paul and other morts. Many morts use ham radios, hidden in cellars and attics, as part of their communication networks. From his radio, Anthony worked on building relationships with the morts.

"Hopefully, one day, they will forgive us and work with us as partners." Anthony remarked one evening as he and Ruth sat on their deck watching the sky grow dark above the dense forest that surrounded them. A loon called in the distance. Woooo, woooo.

Anthony and Mike took a couple of trips from the island to meet with Paul. The trips were risky. There were warrants for their arrest, except for Ruth. Paul had told her that she was becoming a folk hero among the morts, a proto resistance fighter. Despite all of Anthony's planning and foresight, the group still needed last-minute items. It also gave Anthony a chance to learn more about the current situation on the mainland.

Once the living spaces were fully habitable, the group settled into routines. Shifts were devised to keep watch at the camp; two people at all times patrolled the area and the docks. Anthony strongly encouraged them to keep up their weapons training and to have security protocols in case of emergency or invasion. Ruth and Melissa continuously improved their plan to optimize the stores. They had enough canned food and staples, such as rice, but limited protein. They had the others gather as much fruit as they could and harvested what they could from the meager garden. Tessa found mushrooms and after a long bout of research on the datapads to learn if they were edible — they were — the group collected mushrooms to add to the stores.

It was too late in the season to grow much in the garden other than some quick growing vegetables such as spinach and carrots. Ruth and Melissa had big plans for the following spring. They talked dreamily about potatoes, beans, peppers, squash, and rows and rows of peas. They discussed how to keep the deer and rabbits out of gardens and where to expand.

To tackle the protein issue, the Anvil Island group would have become proficient hunters and fishers. Mike and Rick were tasked with creating animal traps for the rabbits and deer on the island. Anthony, always the man with the foresight, had stockpiled a dozen hunting rifles and bows. Dale and Bruce were tasked with fishing. Fortunately, Mike had experience with hunting and fishing, so he instructed all how to dress a deer or rabbit for cooking and how to fillet fish. Most of the group were squeamish, including

Ruth, but all took the lessons seriously. Their survival depended on it.

"Squirrel can be quite tasty, too." Mike suggested, after demonstrating how to skin a rabbit. Ruth was already queasy as she watched him pull the fur off, exposing the poor creature. It seemed indecently naked. She joined in the choir of groans at the thought of skinning a squirrel.

"Why would you even know that, Mike?" Melissa asked in exasperation.

The days were long and full. They had made a lot of progress in setting up the island as their home. The group had also settled into their communal rituals. They gathered for dinner each night and then lingered either at the supper table or in the large den. A deck of cards would appear or an old board game. Melissa recalled some old games such as gin rummy, and they spent the evening amiably.

Some in the group would use the communal light to read. Alexandra pored over medical texts and Anthony reread his favourite books. Ruth sometimes brought out a sketch book. She drew the trees, trying to recreate their intelligent design, the way their branches spread out in geometric patterns to collect the sun. She blended colours to capture the sky and the ocean, the clouds and the sunsets and sun rises. It was satisfying to make art again, to be creative.

Life on Anvil Island was vastly different for all of them after decades and decades in the Blackmore compound. It was simpler, more physical, and very exhausting. Everything was hard work, to prepare food, to have water, to keep clean and warm. The nights when Anthony and Ruth were not on security patrol, they often collapsed beside each other on their bed, fully exhausted, and slept deeply. Their first winter, only months away, would be a challenge, but Ruth was optimistic.

Chapter 21

Early in October, Ruth felt off. She was jittery and nausea, especially in the morning. Then, a week or two later, her breasts felt heavier and tender at the touch. It took another week before Ruth suspected she was pregnant. She had resumed menstruation in August, weeks after she recovered from the virus. Menstruation caught her and the other women in the group off guard. They had to improvise for the necessary supplies. But the women adapted to that like all the other new realities in the group's lives.

Ruth's period was irregular, though, and she did not think to track it. She did not think pregnancy was even possible after so long. She was also so busy every day with the new realities of life on the island — gathering wood, checking the generators, making meals, checking the animal traps —

the list seemed endless. Worrying about a pregnancy was the farthest thing from her mind.

By the end of October, Ruth's belly had become round and hard.

"Anthony, I think we are going to have a baby." Ruth finally admitted to him. She had to repeat herself and then explain the symptoms over and over before the news sunk in for Anthony. And then the biggest grin crept onto Anthony's face. He practically looked insane. He grabbed her hands and danced her around their small living room — a crazy jig. This was not like Anthony at all. It was a crazy moment of sheer joy.

The next day, worry sank in as Ruth and Anthony had to think of the practicalities of having a baby on this isolated island with people who lacked any experience with children or babies. It was over two hundred and fifty years since Ruth had held a baby, and this worried her.

The others on Anvil Island were told of the news. Melissa looked very alarmed. If Ruth could get pregnant, so could the other women. A baby boom here on the island would complicate things.

"Oh, I am happy for you, Ruth, but don't get too close to me. I don't want to catch whatever this is. Seriously, I would not make a good mother."

Ruth laughed.

"You are too hard on yourself, Melissa. One day, maybe you will change your mind. And I think you could be a great mother. But yes, I agree, a baby boom right now, on this island, is not a good idea."

Alexandra, the appointed medical officer, was tasked now with improving her knowledge of prenatal care. She took to the task with relish. To have a challenge, a purpose — she practically vibrated with excitement as she weighed and measured Ruth. Alexandra fabricated a crude pregnancy test with the emergency medical kits Anthony stockpiled. Sure enough, Ruth tested positive. Alexandra searched the datapads on the stages of pregnancy and development of fetuses.

Anthony arranged with Paul an emergency supply run; this time it was for condoms and prenatal vitamins.

"I paid dearly for this supply run, Ruth. But if Paul and his people — your family, I should say — did not care about you, I would still be haggling with him."

The winter set in. It began as a mild winter, mostly frozen rain, typical of the west coast. The Anvil Island group all woke to hoar frost one morning. Trees and their branches were captured in clear, brilliant ice and white frost covered everywhere. It looked like magic as they all gathered near the main house to observe the frozen wonderland that was Anvil Island. Ruth acutely noticed the relations that had formed among them. Stephen and Luke were in the main house. Alexandra and James were in cabin number four. Tessa seemed to be in a triangle of sorts with two younger men, Dale and Bruce. Melissa had originally shown interest in Rick but now seemed to hover around Mike. They all tried to be discreet in the matchups and the breakups that had occurred since August. They all tried to pretend not to acknowledge the others and their romantic follies. Ruth felt like she and Anthony, as the de facto the head of this group, were the parents of a household of hormonal teens. They too did their best to not acknowledge the drama lest it became more acceptable. Anthony made eye contact with Ruth and gave her a bemused smile. He observed too the romantic dramas unfolding in the group, too.

Early December, the security patrol, Dale and Melissa, spotted an ancient fishing boat. Panic set in the Anvil Island group. Everyone rushed to gather weapons. The group agreed that Anthony, Dale, and Melissa would make contact. The rest of the group would keep out of sight until the intentions of this strange boat were determined. Ruth was shaking with anticipation. By now she was over four months pregnant and wearing Anthony's sports pants under the oversized parka she found. What would she do if the island was attacked, if those strangers tried to hurt Anthony and Melissa? Ruth tried to recall the plans discussed months ago, something about holding up in the crawl space of the main house. She made a mental note to rehash the emergency plan in a group meeting.

Ruth continued to watch from in the trees, kneeling behind a boulder. Anthony, Melissa, and Dale walked towards the dock. Their weapons were hidden in their coats. It was a grey and bitter day, threatening to either rain or snow.

Two young men jumped nimbly from the rusted boat. The boat appeared to be pre-halt age. Whatever colour it was long faded to grey and brown. Its sides were covered in ancient welds, metal on metal. The men dressed in waterproof jackets and heavy boots. They both appeared to be stalky, shorter than Anthony. Both had two long dark braids appearing from under woolen toques. They spoke with Anthony, Melissa, and Dale for nearly an hour. Ruth could not hear the conversation, just the low tones of their voices. Her back ached and she shifted frequently. Ruth felt the fabric at knees grow damp and chilled. It was strange how her body was morphing during this pregnancy. The extra pounds she gained felt significant on her lower back and her left hip ached constantly. As she kneeled, she grew more aware of the pain and discomfort. Ruth kept her sight on the group conversing. She would do her best to keep Anthony safe and protect their home. She leaned her rifle against the boulder; a round was chambered and ready.

The conversation appeared to end as the one of the men turned towards their boat. Anthony stepped forward and shook their hands vigorously. Everyone appeared to be smiling. The strangers jumped on their boat as nimble as before. Soon the ancient boat started to cough out black smoke out of its ancient smokestack and moved away.

Anthony, Melissa, and Dale walked towards the cabins, heading towards the main building. Ruth continued to stay hidden from the shore in case the boat occupants could see her. When the boat disappeared from view, the group all gathered at the main building, anxious to hear about the visitors.

"They were fishers from up north, on Haida Gwaii. They are part of the Haida Gwaii First Nation." Anthony explained.

Ruth had not seen any First Nations people since before the halt. She had understood that many of the First Nations on the West Coast were gone from their homes and lands, pushed out by the corporations and the Council. Survivors were driven to north. Some joined the local mort communities, but the majority of the First Nations homes and towns were vacated. Their culture and people seemed to have disappeared, so Ruth thought.

"They apparently have a decent size community on Haida Gwaii. They are too remote for the Council and corporations to bother with, I guess. They trade fish and lumber with the remote mort communities here."

"What do they want from us?" Rick asked.

"They wanted to sell to us — fish, crabs mainly. Or trade with us. They noticed we've been here for a couple of months. They guessed we are trying to keep a low profile here. They heard about the mort rebellion, war, I should say. We didn't say who we were, but I suspect they realize we are former halted."

The ancient boat returned a couple of days later. The Anvil Island Group agreed to let the fishers enter the camp. Four of them landed this time, all male, including a smaller hunched figure — an elderly man. Two of the men were the same men who already met Anthony. Ruth offered some tea and biscuits at the main house. Soon the four strangers seated at the table with six of the Anvil Island group. Tessa and Dale were out on security patrol; James and Luke were chopping wood. The group went through a lot of wood that winter.

They learnt the elderly man's name, Ed. He was an elder in the Haida community and it was thought to be prudent to bring an elder to this meeting of the two groups. Billy and Joe Kaylii, the fishers who visited days ago, were Ed's grandchildren. The other man was Glen Morris, a family friend. The four were quiet. Ruth thought they appeared ill at ease as they sat at the table stiffly. The four kept stealing glances at the Anvil group. Ruth handed them each a steaming mug of tea and placed a plate of cookies in front of them.

"I'm afraid the cookies are a bit stale." Ruth smiled gently at them. "None of us can bake."

Ed nibbled at one and then placed it down. He seemed to struggle with the hard texture. Ed looked even more ancient in the electric light of the house. He looked older than Anne, his face was hardened into deep crevices of wrinkles. Unlike the other men, who had long, black braids of hair, his hair was white and thinning. He had tied back in a simple ponytail. His dark, crinkled eyes appeared gentle and kind. Ruth immediately liked him.

"No wonder you all are so thin, except maybe you, miss." Ed quipped, eyeing Ruth's belly. Ruth laughed, her hand automatically on top of her bulge.

"I don't mind the cookies." Ruth returned the joke. She suspected the four men were very curious about who they were and why were they on Anvil Island. Perhaps they were the first halted people Ed and his people have seen up close. Ruth was now very self conscious as she looked at her group and then at her feet. She knew she looked a mess, again wearing Anthony's sweater and pants. All the Anvil Island members looked a little worse for wear. Their hair was overgrown and the men unshaved. Ruth's own hair always felt dirty; she struggled to keep it clean in the winter months without a proper shower. None of them knew how to cut and style hair. Their previously pampered bodies were sore and underfed as they were long tired of canned or dried food and rice nearly every day. Their skin was red and cracked. Their wardrobes now were about warmth and comfort. All except Ruth had to tighten their belts. Overall, Ruth imagined that these four men looked at her and the others and saw clearly how the Anvil Island group was struggling on their own.

"Miss, I do not mean to pry, but how old are you? Are you a halted?" Ed asked Ruth. He finally looked her in the eyes, curious.

"How old am I?" Ruth realized the fact that she and her group were halted was what intrigued them more than their bedraggled appearances. Ruth decided to be honest. "I am two hundred and eighty-one years old. I don't know how much you know about the conflict on the mainland or about the virus. The virus created to target the halted and start up aging? We were halted, but that is not the case anymore. All of us were infected with that virus and restarted aging. Me, I am having a child too, as you can see."

Ed murmured, taking in the information. He was particularly interested in Ruth, maybe because she was the one most willing to engage with Ed. The rest, the Anvil

Island group and the three men, remained quiet, still wary of each other. To fill the awkward silence, Ruth kept talking and soon found she was telling her life story. It poured out — about Marco and Molly, her job at LIFETECH, how they struggled, how Marco joined the resistance movement. She described that night when LIFETECH was on fire and how Marco died. Ruth felt her face go red when she realized the others were listening intently and looking at her with wide eyes, especially Anthony and Melissa. Anthony's hand moved to her shoulder, a gesture of support. Ruth never told these stories before, not even to Anthony, but she trusted Ed and wanted him and his men to trust her.

The meeting of the two groups ended after several cups of tea and several hours of conversation. Most of the group had opened up and shared their own stories. Ruth heard about life on Haida Gwaii — how several of the first nations banded together there and avoided the reach of the Council. The Haida Gwaii nation was too insignificant or too much trouble for the corporations. LIFETECH and others just ignored them, leaving Haida Gwaii alone. The corporations had other forests and islands, and other morts, to exploit.

Melissa added to the conversation and said a little about her pre halted life — how her parents struggled to support her and her brother, James; they were often hungry. The other formally halted were humbled by Melissa's and Ruth's stories, especially Anthony, but they too shared personal stories. Anthony talked about how he had visited this island as a kid. Ed was particularly interested in this and asked many questions about what the area was like back then, before the halt.

A week later, Billy and Joseph brought a batch of freshly caught crab and a large bag of potatoes. Anthony offered to pay. He waved a spare datapad towards them, hoping it would be a fair trade.

"Next time, when you are more settled. Ed wanted to gift you this. Welcome to the neighbourhood sort of thing," Joseph declined Anthony's offer cheerfully.

The crabs were a hit with the Anvil Island. Ruth boiled them up in the main house and Anthony opened a couple of bottles of wine — precious bottles he was hording for a special occasion. Ruth could not share the wine, but she enjoyed the freshly cooked crab. She marvelled that Anvil Island now had allies in the world. She had allies.

Chapter 22

In the new year, a cold snap settled in for a couple of weeks. The winds off the ocean were bitter, piercing through to the skin. Someone found a box of old ratty wool blankets, grey with ancient mystery stains. Soon they all moved around the island, bundled in the blankets like some strange religious order. Ruth layered up her socks and stuffed her feet into an extra pair of Anthony's boots as she shuffled along on her perimeter walk. Anthony wanted to exclude her from some duties such as security patrol because of her progressing pregnancy.

"Anthony, I am fine. The exercise is good for me. Besides, the others will resent me. I think some of them are not thrilled that we are bringing a baby into the mix. I need to do my fair share."

April came, and Ruth was huge. Alexandra estimated Ruth was over seven months pregnant and due mid May. Ruth could not run now — walking alone with her enormous belly was a significant effort — and she had to give up some of her chores, like chopping wood. Her night shifts were mercifully shortened. Anthony insisted now he would do them. She was restless though, so she settled for leisurely slow-paced walks, and Anthony joined her often. Together, they circumnavigated the entire island. Anthony would talk about plans for the future: a solar farm here, wind turbine there, water collection.

Anthony also discussed what he learnt through the daily radio communications. The world outside seemed to move forward without them. The mort resistant groups continued to make headway. A coalition government of sorts was formed, not quite as Anthony dreamt of, where he had a lead role, but a coalition among the morts. The few halted ones who avoided getting ill, moved to remote compounds, and sealed themselves away, fearful and in denial that their empire was at an end.

The world was changing; the halt was ending; Ruth turned that idea in her head over and over. Reports indicated that the virus was spreading further into Asia and Africa. Mort rebellions and actual full-blown wars were occurring globally. It would take decades, Anthony thought, before the morts were free across the globe, and maybe they would never be free in some areas. Maybe mort overlords would replace the halted overlords. Conflict and power struggles seemed to be the only true constants in human history. So, Anthony slowly shifted his focus to the island, to Ruth and the baby. He had changed; Anthony laughed and smiled more. He visibly worried and fretted aloud; before Anthony hid his emotions behind a cool, confident front. Anthony overall was more human and almost unrecognizable from that self-assured, elegant man he was. Everyday Ruth marvelled how he took part in the new reality of the Anvil Island group: he chopped wood, carried countless buckets of water from the ancient well, and even tried to help at mealtimes. A lifetime of changes in under a year had occurred.

In May, Paul came to visit. He brought Anne with him and her oldest daughter, Karen. Karen was a trained midwife, like Anne. She and Anne insisted on coming to Anvil Island to help. Anthony offered to put the two women up in the main house. Alexandra latched on to Karen, insisting Karen tell her everything about childbirth and births Karen helped with. Anne clucked after the rest in the main house, reorganizing the cupboards and cleaning everything she could. She then tackled the gardens, enlisting Melissa, Dale, and Bruce to be her assistants. Anne had bought baby items, mostly clothes and blankets, for Ruth.

"Go rest Ruth, you won't get as many chances when the baby arrives." Anne shooed Ruth back to her cabin. Ruth surrendered and took a blissful nap. Sleeping at night these days was difficult. Ruth often woke to false contractions — Braxton Hicks, as she recalled — and restless legs. She felt the growing mass of the baby pressing on her bladder and against her ribs, moving mysteriously.

Paul and Anthony set up at the kitchen table in the main building and discussed the state of the world. Anthony recalled the conversation later that evening to Ruth.

"The trials start at the end of July. Many people want the halted to hang. Blackmore especially." Paul reported.

Anthony grimaced. Would they come for him? How could he defend himself considering all that time he was an active member of LIFETECH and the council?

"Paul, what do you think will happen?"

Paul cocked his head in thought. "Maybe watching them grow old in prison might win over. It seems like poetic justice."

"What about us at Anvil Island? Do they want us imprisoned too? We were complicit. I can't deny that. I don't think total forgiveness is likely, but I hope for some reconciliation. A lot of the halted want to make amends and be part of a new world, a more just world."

Paul was unable to give Anthony any solid reassurances.

The baby decided to arrive a couple of weeks late. By then, Ruth was very uncomfortable. Her body felt like weighted down and strained at the seams. She insisted, though, on walking every day. She recalled it helped with labour. It definitely helped temper her excitement. Ruth could barely stand herself with her desire to hold the baby in her arms, to know he or she was ok. It was hard for her to wait patiently for the baby's arrival. Then, on the 27th of May, Ruth woke to strong contractions that did would not relent.

"Anthony, I think it is time." She shook him and he jumped up, his usually well-groomed hair dishevelled. Ruth laughed at the look of panic, at his jerky motions. "Well, it's just the start of labour; this could take several hours."

They walked to the main house where Alexandra had converted a bedroom into an examination room of sorts with a bed for sick or injured. Karen checked Ruth over and assured everyone that labour had begun. Karen showed Alexandra how to determine where the fetus was and how to measure the dilation. Their hands pressed intrusively at Ruth.

In that makeshift medical room, they all assumed their roles — Anthony was the nervous father to be, Alexandra the budding intern, and Karen the wise midwife. All of them were immersed in their roles. Ruth felt like she was watching a play or a movie, or that she was a bit player on a stage. She felt strangely detached from the moment. This was her life, Ruth marvelled, reminding herself — these were the people in it. Despite her fears, Ruth felt very thankful in this moment. Her eyes welled up; she could feel the moisture. Anthony saw and thought she was in pain.

"I'm fine, I'm fine. People have babies every day. Even us." Ruth brushed away his concern.

Outside the room, the rest of the Anvil Island group waited and waited. Those on security patrol dropped in frequently between rounds, hoping not to miss the big moment. When the baby, a healthy crying boy, arrived at eleven am that morning, the house sighed with relief and then rejoiced. Someone broke out a bottle of rum — no champaign to be had on the island — and a mix of coffee cups and juice glasses were used to toast the birth.

The baby was named Daniel Bernard Gelinas, names taken from her father and Anthony's father.

Chapter 23

The first weeks of the baby's life were a blur: feed the baby, change the baby, put the baby down to sleep. Baby Daniel was sleeping in a makeshift bassinet — an emptied dresser drawer. It was déjà vu for Ruth. Daniel was her second child — of course, there were over two hundred years in between, but Ruth remembered the endless duties of a parent of a newborn. Daniel was a chubbier baby than Molly, rounder head. He was just as alert as Molly was, Ruth recalled. His dark eyes seemed to absorb everything around him.

Karen was satisfied with Ruth's and the baby's progress. Ruth had recovered fairly easily from the labour and Daniel latched quickly and was a good eater.

"You got this in hand." Karen said approvingly to Ruth.

"I wonder how I am related to this sweet babe. Am I the great niece? Or cousin four times removed? Do I call him Uncle Daniel?" Anne mused over afternoon tea.

Ruth enjoyed her time with Anne. She would miss this woman when she returned to Richmond. Anne and Karen promised to stay until the end of summer. They enjoyed working with the Anvil Island Group, sharing their knowledge with them.

Anthony did his best to be involved with the baby. He changed and washed diapers. At night he walked circles in the cabin, patting the baby's back when Daniel was fussy.

"I feel a little useless. I don't know what to do, unlike you, Ruth." Anthony admitted to Ruth. He was changing a diaper. He insisted Ruth should sit and rest. Ruth sat on the edge of the bed, but she found it hard to just relax and let Anthony be with the baby. He always seemed a bit frightened near the baby.

"This seems to be natural to you, Ruth, but I want to do my share. I am the. Oh boy." Anthony's face paled. The baby, free of the dirty diaper, started to pee. A arc of urine hit Anthony's sleeve.

"Quick, cover him!" Ruth laughed. This was new to her. Molly had never peed up into the air, though a naked baby Molly peed on Ruth in a doctor's office.

Ruth had a lovely visit one day with Ed and his grandsons. A tiny elderly woman accompanied them. Her thin bent body was covered in clothes too big – a leather belt cinched them in – and her white fizzy hair obscured most of her wrinkled face. She smiled shyly at Ruth and the baby; her brown eyes were gentle like Ed's.

"My wife Dorrie." Ed introduced the woman. Ruth held her hand and was surprised by the power in the small woman's grip.

"Pleased to meet you." Ruth said. Dorrie smiled wider and motioned to hold the baby. In the old woman's arms, Daniel cooed solemnly, mesmerized by the ancient face.

Dorrie and Ed brought a tiny pair of moccasins for the baby, tan suede, with a beautifully beaded pattern on each tiny shoe.

"Oh Ed, Dorrie. These are so beautiful." Ruth hugged the old man; he had a solid presence despite his small stature. Dorrie grinned up at Ruth and then returned her attention to the baby in her arms.

"My daughter also made some baking. She wrote the recipe for you." Ed replied.

August came and Paul came to collect Anthony. There was to be a tribunal, and Paul was to represent himself and the Anvil Island group. Ruth feared the morts wanted retribution. It would not be enough that Anthony aided in the revolution and that he financed the creation of the anti-halting virus. She held on to him tightly before he left with Paul, trying not to cry.

"I'll be fine, Ruth. Especially if I know you and Daniel are here, safe."

Ruth watched the boat motor away from the Island. She let her tears fall free. Daniel squirmed in her arms; he would be demanding to be fed soon. Ruth wiped her face with her free arm and headed back to the cabin.

One night Ruth was sleeping in the cabin, alone in the bed. Anthony's side was cool and empty; he was gone for just over a week. The baby was sleeping in the next room, his breathing loud and rhythmic. Ruth had remarked to Anthony weeks ago how odd it was that a small human could make so much noise when he slept. Ruth slipped into a dream. It was an odd dream — Ruth was in her old apartment that she shared with Marco. Molly was there, six years old and sweet. Baby Daniel was there too. But no Marco, no Anthony. She was feeding the two children, wondering where Marco was. Or was she waiting for Anthony? The phone rang.

"Baby, things went wrong, very wrong. You need to pack up the kids and go." It was Marco's voice, dim and faded. Ruth heard the desperation, the fear. Something bad was happening. The phone cut to a busy sound.

"Marco? Marco? Anthony?" Ruth woke, confused. The familiar cabin room, simple and homey, comforted her. Ruth noticed the sheets on Anthony's side of the bed were still tucked in tight; she recalled he was away. She felt a pang of worry. Anthony had radioed earlier that day to say things were going okay. Some morts still wanted to persecute Anthony and the halted groups that assisted the rebellion. They wanted some period of incarceration, but

Paul had managed to persuade them to consider formal apologies and reparations.

"Don't ask how much. They seemed to overestimate how much I squirreled away." Anthony concluded. Ruth knew Anthony was terrified of losing his safety net. He had never struggled with a lack of money.

Ruth got out of bed to get a drink of water. Through the kitchen window, she saw some movement. It was not a deer or a fox; it was human. Ruth then saw two human figures heading to the main house. She did not recognize them and, by now, she could recognize any of the Anvil Island group from a distance. She kept watching. It was so dark outside. Maybe when they moved closer, she could discern who they were. The moon, hidden under a cloud, emerged and she realized with certainty the two figures were not part of the island group. Strangers. Where was the security patrol? Who was on shift?

Ruth quickly dressed, grabbed the rifle in the front closet. She then gingerly picked up the sleeping Daniel. He protested in his sleep but did not wake. Ruth snuck out of the cabin to Melissa's cabin. Melissa's bedroom was on the far side from the main house and Ruth rapped on the window. Daniel started to fuss, and Ruth hushed him as calmly as she could.

"What are you doing?" Melissa's sleepy voice said, her window opened to the cool night air. Another head popped up beside her; Melissa apparently was back with Rick.

"Shhh, there are strangers heading to the main house." Ruth quickly explained what she saw. She handed Daniel to Melissa through the window. "Lock all the doors and lock yourself in the bathroom with the baby."

"I am coming with you." Rick stated.

"Okay, bring your rifle."

Ruth met Rick at the door of Melissa's cabin. He slipped through the door. Rick called on the cabin next to Melissa's, alerting them to the danger. Rick and Ruth then headed to the main house. By this point, shouting and scuffling could be heard. A woman's scream. Karen? Anne?

Rick and Ruth opened the front door, weapons ready. Two other Anvil Island members, Tessa and Bruce, were outside their cabins, armed and hiding in the shadows.

"Hands up. We are armed!" Rick yelled. They saw Karen and Mike struggling with the two figures near the kitchen. Anne was standing off to the side, holding a kitchen knife. The dining area showed evidence of a fight; the table was askew, and chairs toppled over. Ruth and Rick had startled everyone, especially the unknown intruders. Mike and Karen pushed back the two strangers and moved to Rick and Ruth. Karen brought Anne, shielding Anne with her body. One intruder lunged forward towards Karen and Anne; he too was armed. Ruth, without hesitation, fired her weapon and the unknown intruder dropped to the floor, dark red blood pooling.

"Drop your weapon, hands up." Rick barked at the second intruder. The man dropped his weapon and raised his hands. Ruth recognized him as a halted from Blackmore's compound.

"What are you doing here?" She yelled, moving towards him, weapon aimed at his torso. He refused to talk.

Shots rang out - gunfire from outside, near the front of the main house.

"Mike and I will deal with it. Karen, Alexandra, get some rope and tie him up." Rick motioned for Mike to join him. Karen searched a closet for rope, and then another. Finally, she found rope by the side door. Karen and Alexandra promptly tied the intruder to a kitchen chair. Anne pointed a handgun at him, his own handgun, retrieved from the floor.

Ruth then was surprised to see Alan Blackmore walk into the main house, bloodied and clutching his shoulder. Dale and Bruce had their weapons pointed at him.

"We caught him with another one. Bruce shot both of them. The other one didn't survive," said Dale.

"What are you doing here?" Ruth yelled at him; her fear turning to anger. Alan looked into her, sneering. It looked like he had suffered a gunshot injury on his shoulder, as he was bleeding.

"You bitch. I should have let you die that day. Should have killed you a thousand times over." Alan snarled at Ruth.

"Your ego won't allow it; you needed me around to feed it." Ruth replied.

Dale pushed Alan towards the other intruder, tied to a kitchen chair. Karen grabbed more rope.

Ruth was anxious to get back to the baby. She started to move to the main door and Alan grabbed at her. They both fell to the floor. He kicked and punched at her, then tried to wrap his hands around her neck. Ruth had spent decades training, pushing her muscles and strength as far as she could. She knew Alan had little interest in fitness; she was the stronger one. Ruth fought him back with little effort and got back on her two feet. He grabbed at the weapon she dropped during their fall and struggled to pick it up. She kicked it away; it moved just out of Alan's grasp. Rick yelled at Alan to stay still and when Alan reached for the weapon a second time, Rick fired his rifle at Alan, hitting him in the chest.

"Go, Ruth, go to Daniel." Rick urged her, "We can handle this."

Ruth looked at Alan Blackmore, crumbled on the floor, not moving. She then rushed out of the building.

Daniel and Melissa had remained in the bathroom in Melissa's cabin. Ruth ran from the Main House to the cabin as fast as she could in the dark; her heart pumped loudly in her ears.

"Melissa, open up! All clear! Melissa, it's me!" Ruth struggled with her words, her adrenaline surging. Melissa opened the cabin door with Daniel in her arms. Daniel was howling. He reached out his arms, arching his body away from the frazzled Melissa. Ruth grabbed him and started to cry, too.

"It was Alan Blackmore, Melissa." Ruth said. Her body shook as she held her son.

Melissa embraced Ruth and the baby; all three were crying now. Alexandra entered the cabin. She checked for injuries and told them Alan Blackmore was dying. She confirmed there had been four intruders in total. Two were dead, the other still tied to the chair and Alan, the fourth, was unresponsive. Ruth, clutching Daniel, followed Alexandra and Melissa to the main house.

At the main house, Karen and Anne fussed over the baby as the rest of them stood around the tied-up intruder. Alan was confined in the medical room. He was unconscious and Alexandra thought he would not last long. Blood pooled where Alan was shot and formed a trail towards the medical room.

The intruder, a staffer at LIFETECH — Melissa identified him immediately — told all what he knew. Alan had bribed his way out of prison days ago. He gathered a small crew and headed to the island. Apparently, Ruth and Melissa were tagged with electronic trackers at the back of their necks. This was immediately upsetting to both women.

Melissa let out several expletives. Alan figured Anthony had a safe house and the women's trackers would lead him to it. He hoped to kill Anthony and Ruth and then cause some trouble out of spite. Fortunately, none of his crew had any practical experience with inflicting violence without their mort security.

Ruth tried to reach Anthony by radio. She tried to contact Paul. The unidentified voice on the other end was not helpful.

Melissa and Ruth had Alexandra remove the trackers immediately. It was unlikely anyone other than Alan cared where the two women were, but they were insistent on getting rid of the last shackles of Alan Blackmore.

Alan died by morning. Ruth and Melissa stood silently together in the room, confirming for themselves that he was finally gone. Alan never presented much of a physical threat — his pale body was soft with undeveloped muscles, and he looked ridiculous on close examination with his fine hair combed to cover his perpetual bald spot. Still, Ruth could not look at him without the intense tightness in her chest; she hated that man and everything he represented.

In the morning, Paul radioed back. Anthony was on his way back, he assured Ruth. After lunch, Anthony's boat docked, and Ruth ran to him as soon as he touched land. She needed his embrace. It was clear that Anthony was visibly shaken.

"I should have been here, Ruth. I don't know what I would have done if you or Daniel were hurt. We need to be more serious about defence. Perhaps we can convince some of the mort community to be allies. Like Ed and the rest of Haida Gwaii. We need their experience. We need help." Anthony said.

Later, back in their bedroom, Anthony updated Ruth about the tribunal.

"The conclusion of the tribunal is next week. I need you and Daniel to attend. Paul thinks it will help garner some mercy. We will leave Melissa and maybe Tessa and Dale behind to watch the property. Hopefully, Karen is still willing to stay for a little longer."

Chapter 24

The tribunal was set up like an old court trial in the old city town hall. It reminded Ruth of long ago when she and Marco went to get their marriage licence. Down the hall from the clerk's service window, was the courtroom. Lawyers in their black robes rushed to and from. The mort community had trained lawyers. After all this time? Ruth learnt later they were informally trained, apprenticed through the generations.

The jury or judges — Ruth had only a rudimentary understanding of their roles — were nine persons dressed in their everyday clothes. All were morts, she could tell, hardened by an unforgiven life under the Council. The panel of judges sat imposingly at the front. Massive wooden tables hid their bodies.

Ruth had carefully dressed, simple and sombre, reminiscent of the old outfits she wore pre-halt to LIFETECH. Daniel, almost four months old, wore a typical baby onesie, the nicest one she could find, with matching leggings and a light sweater. The outfit was a gift from Anne. As Ruth and Daniel sat in the area designated for the general audience, Daniel gurgled and laughed, pleased to see new people and a new place. The morts sitting around him were not immune to his charms. She saw people waving their fingers at him and shooting him secret smiles.

Anthony was one of several others to be presented to the tribunal. It was late morning before he presented his case. He stepped up to the podium. Daniel saw him and screamed with joy, bouncing on Ruth's knee. Ruth tried to hush him.

Anthony made his plea to the court.

"I know I will never fully understand the hardships and injustice inflicted on you and your communities, or to Ruth, my partner." All eyes seemed to be on Ruth and the baby; her face felt hot from the attention. Her relation to Paul and his family in the settlement was well known, as well as her captivity at the Blackwell compound. Paul reminded her that everyone had heard the stories about her involvement in the LIFETECH fire centuries before.

"It took me a long time to acknowledge to myself what we did at LIFETECH. I acted too late to stop LIFETECH and the Council. I should have done something sooner. I have no right to ask for mercy, but I am doing so. Please know that I deeply regret my role in the suffering of your communities and wish to continue to make amends. I want to help in moving forward to a more just world."

After Anthony's speech, Paul and Anne appeared on the stand, one after another. Ruth did not know that Anne was here; she found out Anne insisted on attending. Anne and Paul spoke on behalf of the Anvil Island Group and how Anthony funded the anti aging virus and assisted the mort resistance.

"Ruth and Daniel are my family, and so is Anthony Gelinas. They are good people." Anne concluded.

The tribunal did show some mercy. Anthony and his group, including Melissa, were able to remain on the island, but they had to pay reparations. The remaining properties of Anthony were forfeited and divided up amongst the mort communities. The group could remain on the island. Ruth knew though Anthony had stockpiled gold, jewellery, and other valuables in several locations, mostly on the island. He still had a reserve. He had shown Ruth weeks ago where some valuables were hidden, just in case. Anthony was a survivor, just like Melissa, just like herself. He kept what he could for an uncertain future.

The court sentenced Anthony, and other formerly halted individuals who aided the resistance, to decades of community service. They were to assist the mort communities built a better world — a working government, infrastructure, educational institutes. That wasn't a harsh punishment. Frankly, all of them looked forward to the challenge and the opportunity to flex their mental muscles and grow and evolve. Wars still raged in the east and to the south. The mort communities were not all in a mutual agreement of how to proceed in a new world without the halted.

In September, Ruth and Melissa planned a gathering. It would be a celebration of the end of the tribunal, and a new beginning for the Anvil Island Group. Ruth and Melissa planned invitations for Paul, Anne, Karen, as well as Ed and his family. The two women enthusiastically discussed the menu. Roast venison and fish for the meat dishes were obvious choices. Thanks to Anne's supervision, the garden had done very well that summer and would provide a variety of vegetables for the celebration. Tessa and Dale were experimenting with baking and have made a lot of progress into pies and cakes. It would be, the two women agreed, a great party, a chance to give back to those who helped them establish a new life at Anvil Island.

"It's just like the Thanksgiving dinners we use to have," Ruth said, "I use to love Thanksgiving weekend. It was family just getting together and eating."

Melissa stared blankly at Ruth. She had never heard of the holiday. Ruth thought hard on how to explain Thanksgiving.

"The holiday began in the United States when the settlers – pilgrims – arrived in North America and nearly starved. The First Nations helped them and they had a feast. Roast turkey. The United States held their holiday in November but Canada held theirs in October, closer to the end of the harvest. As a girl, my mom always made the best gravy and mashed potatoes. I loved roast turkey and gravy. And then we would have pumpkin pie. We'd go for a walk in the park and enjoy the fall colors. It was just a simple holiday – a day to be thankful."

"I never heard of this. It sounds nice." Melissa replied. "My parents were always working. We never seemed to be all together. If they had a day off, usually, just an afternoon, it was such a rare occasion. We'd go to the beach then. My brother and I would dig out forts in the sand or try to catch crabs." The two women were silent, lost in the memories of their childhoods.

"I think though we have a lot to be thankful here. This island, our lives together. We should celebrate that." Melissa spoke, breaking the silence.

"Okay, let's bring back Thanksgiving." Ruth replied. Melissa nodded.

A week later Anvil Island hosted its first celebration. It was a simple affair – good food, good company. Ed brought his children and grandchildren and great grandchildren. Dorrie also came, insisting on holding Daniel for most of the visit. Paul, Anne and Karen arrived with a few of their own family. After dinner, they gathered on the rocky shore by the docks and lit a campfire. Musical instruments came out; songs, stories and laughter filled the evening. The light of the fire, orange and red, danced up to the darkening sky and reflected in the faces of the Anvil Island Group and their guests. Ruth held a sleepy Daniel and leaned into Anthony. Daniel yawned, fighting against sleep. He didn't want to miss a thing. His eyes followed the group of children, Ed's great grandchildren, as they hollered and ran down the shore.

Ruth surveyed the faces around the fire. Most people were huddled in jackets as they conversed as the evening grew chilly. Many were bundled in the old grey blankets from last winter. Something was different, Ruth thought. She watched Melissa grin wide as Mike told a joke. Melissa, without her makeup and her styled hair, was still a beautiful woman, perhaps more so, Ruth thought. Ruth looked then at Dale and Tessa. Everyone looked different somehow. Their faces appeared youthful despite the long cool day and a hard year on the Island. Even Ed and Anne seemed years younger. Then, it dawned on Ruth, the tension of the past year, the past decades, was broken. There was now hope and moments of happiness, even for herself.

Chapter 25

Fifty years after the mort resistance at Blackmore Compound, Ruth woke in her bed, confused from the dreaming world that gently held her captive. The sun seeped in through the edges of the curtained window and slowly lit the room as it rose higher. It was a modest room; the bed took up most of the space. A well-worn quilt, colourful patterned squares, and the occasional patched spot covered the bed. Across from the bed was a large wooden dresser. A series of framed picture garnished the top. Without her glasses, Ruth could not make out any detail of the photos, except maybe a pair of eyes and the shape of a head. She blinked and rubbed her eyes, and fully came into herself, fully awake if not fully alert. She was in the bedroom that was nearest the kitchen.

Ruth struggled to rise out of bed. Arthritis invaded her shoulders and hip, and it was at its worse in the morning.

Every year, the stiffness and pain grew worse. The pain was particularly sharp on the left side because of old injuries. She pushed herself up with her right arm and gingerly swung her legs over. Ruth shuffled her feet into slippers. The wood floor of the room was always cold, even in summer. It was April, and the mornings were still chilly. With considerable effort, Ruth rose from the bed. She stretched out her arms and shifted her body around to loosen up her joints, and Ruth then headed to the washroom outside her bedroom. She knew from experience that once she got moving, the pain would retract a bit and her mobility would improve. Before she left the room, Ruth opened the curtain and the April sunshine gently invaded, casting its warm glow fully in the room and on the walls. Ruth's paintings, mostly of the island and the ocean, reflected the golden light; paint stokes glowed and sparkled in the streams of sunlight.

The bathroom, too, was modest — a toilet, a cabinet, a sink, and a mirror. The big luxury was the white enamel tub. It was installed forty years ago when the house was constructed and it held up pretty well over the decades, suffering a few scratches and water stains. The showerhead on the wall was installed afterwards once the island well was enlarged and Anthony was able to procure electric water pumps for the Anvil Island residents. Hot running water from a tap! That was a great day of excitement for Ruth and the other islanders.

Ruth used the toilet and washed up at the sink. All these years and she still marvelled at the concept of running hot water, the sensation of warm water flowing over her hands and in between her fingers — effortless and luxurious. She stared into the mirror, slightly tarnished with age, and saw the face of an eighty-year-old. It was always a bit of a shock to see an older woman in the mirror — the wrinkles, the grey hair, the watery eyes. Ruth was well over three hundred and twenty years old and in relatively good health for an eighty-year-old woman, but she had developed high cholesterol and struggled with her potassium level. Ruth also had to admit that she found increasingly that her brain felt muddled. She mixed up names of people and frequently forget words. She felt stalled, like she was falling behind, while everyone and everything around her moved forward. Still, she was proud to have made it to this point through so many decades with her body and mind relatively intact. Surely, she could be allowed to slow down at her age.

Life on Anvil Island had been pretty good to her. Ruth and Anthony remained on the island all this time, though Anthony was often pulled away from the island for business. He was the chief financial officer for the Coalition government for decades until his aging body forced him to retire. Ruth also worked, though she stayed mostly on the island. She worked in the Coalition's education ministry, compiling and editing educational materials for the emerging schools. She got the chance to tour the schools on the mainland several times and she loved interacting with the children. It was a dream job; Ruth felt she made a difference and there were the children. She loved to see so many children in a classroom, to hear their excited chatter, and to watch their perpetual motion; she relished their zest for life.

Anthony and Ruth had two more children after Daniel was born, two girls named Holly and Grace. They had to build another home, this house, slightly larger to accommodate the five of them. It was near their little cabin and still modest. They would never live again in the opulence of the halted era. The island population slowly grew to its present-day number of approximately five hundred people and a ferry system was installed decades ago, connecting them to the mainland and to the other island communities such as Haida Gwaii. A small school was built on the island. It started its life as a one room school to accommodate her children and a dozen other children of the Anvil Island group. It slowly grew as the population grew.

Melissa eventually had two children, not with Rick or Mike, but with a mort man she met when she went back home in Chilliwack. Months after the tribunal, Melissa's brother, James, reached out to Melissa. He came to the island to meet her. As the old man embraced the youthful Melissa, the contrast was startling. Ruth still remembers this image of Melissa and her brother holding each other tight, making up for lost time. Melissa left the island for a couple of years to reconnect with her brother and his family.

"Ruth, I cannot believe it. He forgives me for leaving. I can't even forgive myself."

"Go be with your family, but I will miss you, Melissa. Come back and visit anytime; you are always welcome in our home."

Melissa returned to Anvil Island eight years after her departure, now appearing to be in her late twenties. She brought a husband and a toddler and busied herself with the governing of Anvil Island. She helped Anthony oversee the expansion — new houses, the medical centre, the school. Anthony was able to entice some of the mort community to the island, and the trading relations with the Haida Gwaii nation led to marriages and subsequent children.

Thirty years after the birth of Daniel, Ruth and Anthony found themselves alone in the house. The small house seemed large after the children left. Daniel had moved out and was working in the new medical centre on the island, interning as a doctor. The younger children, Holly and Grace, were away, attending post secondary school near the old city of Vancouver. Anthony was long retired, and Ruth was looking forward to her own retirement.

It was a period of optimism. The Coalition made significant improvements to stabilize the Americas. The civil wars to the east had ended five years ago and trade was flourishing across the continent. The future looked bright. Perhaps even grandchildren were a possibility as Daniel was courted a local woman. It was such a far cry from the bleak loneliness of the Blackmore compound. Ruth, looking over her long life, felt blessed to have had two loving partners in her life and four children, stretched through the fabric of time. She still dreamt of Marco and Molly; their ghosts still lived in the back of her mind through her waking hours. In her dreams, her two families — Marco's and Anthony's — blended together seamlessly, crossing boundaries of time.

The fall day was golden as the leafy trees turned red, yellow, and orange. Ruth went for her daily walk. This time she headed out alone, as Anthony was complaining he was not feeling well. Biologically, he was nearing eighty. He had relatively few health issues over the decades, but time was catching up with him. His back and joints were stiff and achy, and he had frequent indigestion. Ruth had struggled with menopause, but now she was on the other side of it, she felt pretty good for being biologically in her sixties.

Ruth saw a herd of the tiny island deer. A red fox ran across her path. Then, high above in the sky, Ruth saw the silhouette of an eagle. Their island was teeming with life. She returned home and called out to Anthony; an eagle is a rare sight near the Anvil town centre.

"Anthony, honey. Where are you?"

No response. "Anthony?"

She found him still in their bed, his complexion grey, eyes closed. She rushed to his side, and he was not breathing.

Daniel rushed to the house with a medic. The two immediately attempted resuscitation while Ruth stood there frozen. Daniel and the medic then loaded him on the medical transport and rushed Anthony to the medical centre. Anthony never gained consciousness. He died that night. Ruth had lost her second husband.

Twenty years later, Ruth stayed in the house; it took a while to get used to the solitary. She initially had to force herself to keep engaged in the community. Her children would not let her withdraw from Anvil Island life, though. Ruth also had her art, her work, and the children at the school where she volunteered at. Eventually, her daughters returned to the island and her middle child, Holly, moved into the house with her own spouse. It made no sense for Holly to find a home when this one was nearly empty.

Slowly, Holly and her growing family took over the house and Ruth found herself moved into a reorganized bedroom on the main floor for the last decade. Ruth was present for the births of Holly's children; she helped with Holly's household, making meals and minding the grandchildren. Ruth became Grandma.

"Mom, just checking on you." Holly knocked lightly on the bathroom door and interrupted Ruth's reverie. Ruth had been peering into the mirror for quite some time. The old woman in the mirror quietly looked back, revealing nothing. It was the only bathroom in the house, so she felt a tinge of guilt for monopolizing it.

Ruth had spent hundred of years looking at, and avoiding, the same unchanging face for hundreds of years. She never thought she would get used to a face that ages with the years. But there was comfort in the changes. Her face and body were road maps to a life that was finally unstuck and unfolding into possibilities she had thought were lost to her.

"Yes Molly. Holly. Coming right out." Ruth cringed a little. Her daughter now will question her mental capabilities. Holly will call the other two and the three of them will go on about how Mom has dementia. Well, after all this time, surely, Ruth can be forgiven if she is a little forgetful. Over three hundred years of moments to remember was a lot, but this generation and the ones to follow would never experience this, hopefully. No person needs to have it all — wealth, time, space — at the expense of vast groups of others. People had to know when to make room for the younger generations, to prop them up and then retreat away slowly so they can live their lives with hope and possibility. Ruth struggled for centuries with the old guilt for surviving so long.

What Ruth would do to forget some things, like Marco's death and life at Alan Blackmore's compound, like the feeling that Molly was out there but Ruth could not find her or help her. Ruth hoped Molly understood Ruth did not abandon her. Those moments, those feelings of sorrow and desperate, still have their hold on Ruth. Other moments, Ruth never wants to forget: family holidays as a child, life with Marco, all the babies, Anthony, the children in the classrooms. Memory was a funny thing. Ruth could remember the old memories better than what happened yesterday, last month, or twenty years ago. She still vividly recalled dancing in the kitchen with Marco on their wedding day and the day she first visited Anvil Island with Anthony.

Ruth sat down at the old kitchen table; the same one Anthony had made when they moved into the house. He was so proud to have made something so solid with his own hands. Holly handed her a plate of eggs, toast, and fruit. Then Holly placed a cup of steaming tea beside the plate. Ruth saw her pills in a small bowl, and she gulped them down obediently. She looked across the table at Holly, who was now seated with her own plate of food. Did she, Ruth wondered, remember to thank her daughter for the food?

Holly got most of her looks from Ruth — grey eyes and dark hair, similar completion. Her height — Holly was taller than Ruth — seemed to be from Anthony's side. Holly would be — Ruth struggled to recall — forty-four. Yes, Ruth was certain Holly was forty-four. A schoolteacher, Ruth was happy to recall, Holly was a schoolteacher; she still was. It was Saturday, so they were having a leisurely day.

Holly also had three children, all boys, aged twelve to six. The house was normally very loud and boisterous. The boys were always running and climbing everywhere and on everything. Holly constantly yelled at the children to go play outside. This morning, the house was quiet. David, Holly's partner, must have taken the boys outside.

After breakfast, Holly helped Ruth put on her jacket and gathered Ruth's purse. Ruth felt she did not need Holly's help, but it was easier to let her children help. Sometimes you had to let others help, Ruth mused. You had to let them in. They walked the short distance to the main house; Holly took one of Ruth's elbows and held it the entire way as if Ruth was fragile or perhaps fearing Ruth would run away. The main house was now a community centre for the small island community. The exterior was recently refreshed. It had new siding and windows, as well as a new roof. It now had a log cabin look, a far cry for all the glass and steel of the Anvil Island Group's arrival. Steel was still difficult to get in this post halt world, especially off the mainland.

Inside the living room was expanded to include several tables and chairs for community members to use for games, crafts, meetings. The kitchen was modernized to allow food preparation for larger groups. The bedrooms were now offices. After the islanders could build a separate medical building, they moved the medical suite out long ago, and Daniel began work as its head medical officer.

The dining area beside the kitchen was changed to host meetings and small public gatherings — like today. Today's event was Ruth's birthday; she turned three hundred and twenty-two years old. She was the oldest person on the island. Anthony, before his death twenty years ago, was the oldest of the Anvil Island Group. Ruth was the first one to be halted, and Melissa was the last to be halted. And there Melissa was, sitting on a chair, one of many chairs positioned along the wall to accommodate the birthday guests. Melissa sat between her spouse, her son, and daughter-in-law. Ruth looked around the room. All her children were there with their partners and own children. Ruth had six healthy, beautiful grandchildren in total.

Paul Foster was there too, slumped over in a wheelchair. His body was withered with age, but his eyes — his eyes still glinted with intelligence, still assessing the situation. Ruth had counted on his friendship throughout the decades. He was always fiercely loyal to her and gave sage advice. He was always her family.

A table was set up, beautiful tablecloth, plates, and knives. In the centre was a birthday cake, iced in soft pastels with large yellow flowers -- her favourite colour. There was one large candle in the centre.

"We don't want to burn the island down with all those candles." Paul struggled to get his words out, and everyone laughed politely. He had a stroke about five years ago, which affected his communication.

"Ha, ha old man. You wish you could look so good as this old woman." Ruth patted his curled hand that gripped the arm of his wheelchair.

One of the grandchildren insisted everyone should sing Happy Birthday. To be honest, Ruth struggled to remember the grandchild's name or age and had to rely on referring to each of them as 'Dear' more that she would have liked to.

There were so many children in her life for the last fifty years. It was a perk of her work — working on curriculum, visiting schools, even teaching in the island school. She loved every moment, especially the interactions with the school children. Parenting with Anthony was hard, especially during the uncertainty of the reconstruction years. Both of them were always worried about something: having enough food, keeping the generators operating, keeping warm and dry in the winters. They stressed over illnesses and injuries. They fretted over the precarious nature of the world. How long would they be able to live in peace on Anvil Island?

Post halt, their life was hard and full of struggle and uncertainty, but she loved every moment. This world allowed her to see people and children grow and develop into their own beings. It truly was an honour to be a part of that. Ruth had experienced the opposite of this for hundreds of years — stuck in an ageless body, alone in a sterile tower.

"Happy birthday, dear Grandma, happy birthday to you." The ancient song concluded. Ruth's smile strained a little through the chorus of voices; her face flushed hot. She never felt comfortable being the centre of attention. But she was happy, happy to see so many familiar and loved faces.

"Blow out the candle, Grandma."

Manufactured by Amazon.ca
Acheson, AB

13979847R00190